Phyllis Clark
and the
Third Eye

by

A. P. Dunar

Chapter One

A Desperate Man

Patterson Steward entered the office of Ricky Rance at the Chicago Tribune newspaper. Rance looked up from his typewriter and stared at the young man questioningly.

"You said that you're doing research for Phyllis Attlee?" Rance sighed. "Her husband, Ben, usually does all her research."

"He's tied up at Olis Ritt University this week, so they asked me to handle it," explained the nervous college student.

"How do you come to know the Attlee's?" Rance probed.

Patterson smiled slightly, "I'm Phyllis' Uncle Henry's teaching assistant."

Rance chuckled faintly, shrugged, and then smiled, "Henry's a real hoot. What can I do for you?"

Patterson relaxed a little, "I've been asked to find out all I can about psychics and clairvoyance."

Rance stopped typing, "That's a pretty tall order."

Patterson nodded.

"Charlatans or true practitioners?" Rance asked.

"Both, actually," answered Patterson.

"And why start with me?" wondered Rance.

"I read your Sunday insert piece and thought that it was interesting," returned Patterson.

Rance shook his head, "I did that nearly two years ago, last Halloween."

"I found it in the library at school. It was a true wealth of information. I was wondering if you still had your notes, and if so, could I see them?" Patterson explained.

"I don't use notes," Rance laughed. "I have an identic memory. It's all floating around in my head."

Patterson looked skeptical.

"What exactly are you looking for? Maybe I can save you some time," Rance inquired.

Patterson glanced around the tiny office nervously, wondering how he should sum up all his questions into one quick response. Rance stared at Patterson in anticipation.

Patterson exhaled hard, "How can you prove to someone that a psychic is not really psychic?"

Rance grinned broadly, "That's assuming that the psychic is not really psychic!"

"But they're not!" protested Patterson.

Rance chuckled, "The ones in the piece that I did were not, but there are indications that some do exist."

Patterson looked dismayed, "Indications?"

"There have been a lot of studies into para-psychology and there is something there," refuted Rance.

Patterson was confused, "But your article…"

"Was written for Halloween", stated Rance, cutting Patterson off. "The entire thrust of it was to play down the evil witch thing," Rance defended.

"Surely you can't believe in all that mumbo jumbo?" argued Patterson.

"Of course not!" returned Rance. "Ninety-nine percent of the people out there are absolute frauds. However, there is that one percent that…"

"You seemed to have a different view two years ago," refuted Patterson.

"I'm just saying that you need to have an open mind about the research that you're doing," Rance sighed. "Yeah, most of the guys running around fleecing old ladies of their money are fakes. But there are people being studied at respectable institutions who seem to be very real."

Patterson stood quietly for a few seconds as Rance returned to his typing.

"How do you tell the real ones from the fakes?" Patterson finally asked.

Rance stopped typing again, "It ain't easy, Kiddo! The first true warning sign is that they ask for money."

"So, if they don't appear to be after money, they are real?" Patterson sneered.

"No!" exclaimed Rance. "You need to get past their tricks."

"Tricks?" questioned Patterson.

Rance lowered his head and shook it, pushed back away from his desk and stood up.

"Ok, I'm a psychic," Rance announced.

Patterson laughed cynically.

"Don't believe me?" Rance chuckled. "You come from a wealthy family, but you no longer live at home. You wear glasses when you read, and you read a lot. You graduated from Mayfair High School in 1973. You smoke a pipe in remembrance of your deceased grandfather, whom you loved dearly. And you ate lunch at Billy Goat Tavern just before you came here. Most likely, you had a hamburger with grilled onions and potato chips. How close am I?"

Patterson was astonished, "Spot on! You are psychic!"

Ricky Rance burst into laughter.

Patterson looked at Rance with annoyance.

"I am not psychic, you fool," Rance hooted. "Here you are, an intelligent college student who apparently does not believe in the supernatural, and yet, in a few seconds I was able to securely plant the seeds of doubt in your mind."

"But how could you know all that about me?" Patterson stuttered.

Rance breathed out a long breath, "Easy! I'm a good reporter. I observe things. You are wearing an expensive wristwatch and high end

Italian shoes, obviously you come from money. Yet, the button down collar on your, also expensive shirt, is only buttoned down on one side. If you were living at home, either a mother or maid would have noticed that and either fixed the other button or removed it from your wardrobe until it was fixed. I can tell that you wear glasses from the indentations on the bridge of your nose and your temples. You're not wearing them now, therefore I would surmise that you need them only to read. You are a student, so you read a lot, as evidenced by those same indentations. Your high school and graduation date are on your senior class ring which you are wearing. You smoke. The smoke stains that are on your teeth attest to that. Smoke and coffee stains just don't come off, regardless of how often you brush. By the way, I didn't mention that you drink a lot of coffee. That's too easy, all students drink too much coffee. I said a pipe, because cigarettes and cigars leave a rather objectionable smell on the smoker's clothes, whereas pipe tobacco is quite pleasant. Most people your age opt for cigarettes, but you did not. You chose the pipe because your grandfather smoked one. I only guessed that it was your grandfather, as I noticed a pocket watch chain hooked to your beltloop. As I said before, you are wearing an expensive wristwatch, therefore the pocket watch is carried, not only to tell time, but also as a remembrance. Pocket watches are a grandfather thing. The fact that you have it, and not your grandfather, would suggest that he has passed away."

"And lunch at Billy Goat Tavern?" wondered Patterson.

Rance snickered, "No offense, but I could smell onions on your breath, the sweet smell of grilled onions, not the sharp smell of chopped. That along with the ketchup spot on your expensive Italian shoe makes me think hamburger. The potato chip crumbs caught on your belt buckle is a dead giveaway. Billy Goat's is the only place around here that serves chips and not fries with their burgers."

Patterson shook his head, "That's absolutely amazing."

"That's not all," continued Rance. "The long red hairs on your jacket lead me to believe that you're dating Nora, the receptionist at Clark investigations. And I would strongly consider that this is your only connection to the Clarks."

Patterson looked distressed, "Yes, I am dating Nora."

"That's only half an answer," pressed Rance.

"Why do you think that I'm not working for the Clarks?" asked Patterson.

Rance snickered, "If you're impressed by my powers of observation, you haven't been around Philip and Phyllis. Either of them would have picked up on a half dozen more tells on you."

Patterson nodded, "You are right."

"Now, why are you really here?" pressed the reporter.

Patterson considered his options carefully. He decided to tell Ricky Rance the truth.

"You're right," Patterson began, as Rance sat down. "I'm not here on the behalf of the Clarks. I have nothing at all to do with them. I do date Nora, their receptionist. Actually, Professor and Mrs. Attlee have taken us out to dinner on one occasion. I'm not really sure why they did that."

Rance nodded, "Phyllis and Ben are good people. And I don't have all day."

"I'm essentially here because my Aunt Mariah Emmerson has come under the influence of a man claiming to be a psychic," confessed Patterson.

Rance frowned, "And you are concerned for her welfare."

Patterson nodded.

Rance sat thinking for a few moments, "Has he taken or asked for any money?"

Patterson shook his head, "No, not that I know of, not that she will admit to."

"Did she first contact him or was it the other way around?" inquired the reporter.

"Shortly after my Uncle Ted passed away, this guy walked up to her in the park one day," answered Patterson.

"Had she ever met him before?" questioned Rance.

Patterson shook his head again, "He just walked up to her and said that he could feel that she was suffering a great loss. He told her that he understood what she was going through and would like to try to help her. My Aunt is not a very religious woman, although she feels that she is spiritual. She was having a difficult time with Uncle Ted's death. At first, she just ignored him, but when he continued to go on about feeling that she had lost someone very close, and then coming right out and mentioning that he felt that it was her husband, Theodore, she broke into tears and sat down on a park bench with the guy. When she asked him how he knew so much, he said that he had the third eye.”

“Yeah, he’s a phony,” agreed Rance. “Professional con artists read the obituaries religiously looking for wealthy women whose husbands have passed away. There usually is way too much personal information revealed in those obits. It makes for easy picking for unscrupulous grifters.”

“She sees this guy almost every day now,” admitted Patterson.

“You said that you’re dating the Clark receptionist, why don’t you just ask Ben Attlee to take a look into the matter?” wondered Rance.

Patterson once again looked disgruntled, “I’m not on the best of terms with any of them right now.”

Ricky Rance scrutinized the young college student carefully. “What on earth did you do to get on the outs with the Clark clan?”

Patterson was unmistakably humiliated and ashamed by the way the conversation was going.

"I told Lieutenant Jack Flynn that I worked for the Clarks and needed to see the case file on the Monday Morning Murderer," confessed Patterson uncomfortably.

Ricky Rance's eyes opened wide, "You did what?"

"I'm a journalism major and I was hoping to get some sort of scoop that I could sell to some newspaper to get my foot in the door," admitted Patterson.

"That wasn't the smartest move," admonished the veteran reporter. "First of all, no reputable newspaper would buy any story like that from an unknown without carefully verifying the source. Also, that could have gotten you locked up! What's more, had you spilled confidential information about the case, the murderer could have gotten away. That's not a very good way to begin your career."

"It gets worse," sighed Patterson.

"I doubt if that's possible," countered Rance.

"I said that I had information from Pauli Boy DeLuca," Patterson related.

"That…that could have gotten you killed!" exclaimed Rance.

Patterson stared humbly at the floor.

"You did all that and then you have the nerve to come in here telling me that you're doing research for the Clarks?" Rance demanded loudly. "What is wrong with you? Didn't you learn your lesson the last time?"

Rance sat at his desk stewing.

"It's just that I need to do something about my Aunt's situation," Patterson offered modestly.

"You obviously come from money, why doesn't your father hire a detective?" requested Rance.

"My parents don't get along with Aunt Mariah. They say that she's everything that they hate," confided Patterson.

"And what's that?" challenged Rance.

"They don't like people that flaunt their money and think that they're better than others," sighed Patterson.

Rance snickered and huffed, "Sounds like I'd like your parents."

"My father says that she's making her own bed, and she'll have to lay in it," moaned Patterson.

Rance leaned way back in his chair and breathed heavily and slowly, "I'd like to help you somehow, kid. But the best advice that I can give you is to eat crow and beg the Clarks to help you!"

It wasn't what Patterson had hoped to hear, but it was his only option.

Chapter Two

Nowhere Left to Turn

It was almost lunch time Tuesday morning August 19th, as Patterson sat in the summer class that he was taking. It was the last week of class, and he had a difficult decision to make. Actually, he had hoped that Duckworth Shetz would have continued as Professor Weatherby's teaching assistant. Patterson had known Duck when they were in high school. He hadn't known Duck well, but then, Patterson hadn't gotten to know very many people well in high school. The fact that he had been a freshman when Duck was a senior just made matters worse. Duck had been posing as Henry Weatherby's assistant while he was working undercover on a case.

Patterson figured that, since he had some distant connection with Duck, it would be easier for him to talk to him about the situation with his Aunt. He wondered if maybe Duck and Jackie might be able to look into it on their own. He knew that the two were apprentices at the Clark detective agency, but he really didn't know how that worked. It didn't really matter, as Duck wasn't around anymore since the case that he'd been working on had come to completion.

Because of Patterson's relationship with Nora, he was well aware that his teacher, Doctor Henry Weatherby, was Phyllis Clark's uncle. Weatherby and Nora were Patterson's only connection to the Clark agency. Nora was very aware of the stupid stunt that he had tried to pull with the police department. Because of it, he was on thin ice with her concerning anything to do with her job. He wondered how much Professor Weatherby knew about it, if anything.

Patterson was mulling this all over in his mind as this day's class drew to a close. This was the last week of class and after that he would have only Nora to link him to the help that he so desperately desired for his aunt. As the bell rang, signaling the end of class, all the students rushed out of the lecture hall except for Patterson. Doctor Weatherby noticed the young man and asked him if there was something that he could do for him. Patterson said that there was.

Weatherby invited the student to his office, expecting that he was having some difficulty with the course material. He was surprised at what he was about to hear. Patterson outlined the story pretty much as he had told it to Ricky Rance.

Henry Weatherby sat quietly listening to the tale.

"That's quite a dilemma you're carrying around young man," Henry offered. "But I don't understand why you're telling all this to me, unless you just needed to talk about it?"

"I've read your books and I know about your connection to the Clark Detective Agency," advised Patterson.

Henry furrowed his brow, "I see. You know, there are some responsible psychics and spiritualists out there. Perhaps, it would be wise if we set up a meeting with one of my fellow professors. Doctor Stan Kole is a noted psychologist and physicist whose specialty is investigating para-normal activity. He's done a lot of work with psychics. He knows who's on the level and who's not, and he knows how to deal with them."

Patterson was relieved and excited about Henry's suggestion. Henry arranged for them to meet with Kole the next day after class.

Patterson went away feeling much better than he had in some time.

That evening Patterson picked up Nora from work. The two went to dinner together. Nora had become worried about Patterson, not just because of the abnormal interest that he had shown in the Monday Morning Murderer serial killer, but in general. She'd gone to high school with Patterson. However, she hadn't seen him in the two years since their graduation until they ran into each other at the beginning of that summer. Since that chance meeting at the Chicago Art Institute, the two had started seeing each other on a regular basis. Nora had remembered Patterson as a very serious person in high school. In high school, Patterson was thought of as being dark and strange. But Nora had found that he had a fun side also. Yet, in the last few days, she could tell that there was something bothering him. Of course, Nora was totally unaware that his Uncle Theodore had passed away on August 8th. Today, he seemed much happier, that is, if you could call what he ever was as "happy" at all.

Nora looked at her boyfriend as they ate, not able to help but wonder what was going on in his strange, twisted mind. She just had to ask.

Patterson told Nora about the death of his uncle and what was going on with his aunt. Then he added that he had an upcoming meeting with Doctor Kole.

Nora expressed how sorry she was that his uncle had passed away, adding that she was upset that he hadn't told her about it sooner. She said that she would have liked to be there for him at the funeral. Patterson thanked her and added that he had been alright with it. It was the fact that his aunt was being taken in by a con artist that was worrying him.

"You know, had you not done what you did with Lieutenant Flynn, I bet that Phyllis would have had Duck and Jackie help you out," Nora chastised.

Nora had opened the door.

"Do you think that Duck and Jackie could look into it anyway?" Patterson begged.

Nora was upset that Patterson even had the nerve to pose such a thing. Patterson argued that it wasn't for him, but for his poor widowed aunt. Nora was a compassionate person and considered how she would feel if it was a member of her family who was being taken advantage of in such a way. Even though she wasn't happy about going to bat for Patterson, she decided that, since it was only Jackie and Duck that she would be asking, she would do it.

On Wednesday, August 20th, Patterson ran laps on the university track, showered, and then went to Professor Weatherby's class, as he had been doing everyday of the summer. For the first time since this whole thing started with his aunt, Patterson was filled with encouragement. Enthusiasm and eagerness were emotions quite distant and unfamiliar to Patterson, although that is exactly what he was feeling as Professor Weatherby's class ended and he joined Henry for the walk over to Doctor Kole's office.

Doctor Kole was a very tall, slender, young man. Although not especially handsome, he was not strange or unnerving in his features or actions. Patterson hadn't had any idea of what to expect, but somehow, he'd envisioned that a professor who specialized in the study of the para-normal would look and act ghoulish and weird. Doctor Kole looked and acted more normal than Henry Weatherby, but that was easy.

Doctor Kole greeted the two men cordially and offered them coffee. They sat down together.

"Doctor Weatherby has informed me of the general nature of your problem concerning your aunt," Kole began. "I hate to jump to any instant conclusions, but my first gut feeling is that this man that Doctor Weatherby told me about is most likely a fraud. I know that, of all people, I shouldn't be saying that, but true psychics are unfortunately rare, whereas, frauds are not. And just as unfortunately, the frauds are very successful, particularly in a case like your aunt's, when the person is actually eager to believe them."

"I don't understand how she could let herself fall victim to a guy like this," commented Patterson.

"I take it that your uncle died unexpectedly?" considered Doctor Kole.

Patterson nodded, "Yes, he was exercising in his gym and suffered a fatal heart attack."

"You'd be surprised at how many people die exercising. That's why I avoid it at all costs," added Henry Weatherby.

"When the bereaved have a great deal of time to prepare for the death of a loved one, they get ready for it, both emotionally, and practically. Of course, there is always that sense of unbearable loss. However, there are no loose ends to be concerned over. Usually, all business matters have been finalized. In the case of a surprise death, there are things that the deceased may have never even thought to discuss with is or her spouse. For instance, they might not have discussed the safety deposit box where the bonds and insurance policies are kept," disclosed Doctor Kole. "And then there are sometimes those things that surface that were deliberately kept a secret."

Patterson looked dismayed, "I understand."

"Because of all of these things, not to mention the emptiness felt, the spouse is panicked and feels driven to find answers. Hence, enters your friendly psychic, who offers to find all the answers, with the added factor of being able to say that one last 'goodbye, I love you'." Kole added, "It's heart breaking and, oh, so easy."

"How do I get Aunt Mariah to recognize all this?" begged Patterson.

"Well, first of all, you need to absolutely establish the fact that this psychic is indeed a fake, which he probably is. Your aunt needs to be educated before you can even begin to challenge the authenticity of her psychic," proposed Doctor Kole.

"I don't think that will be easy," sighed Patterson.

"The fact that you are in Doctor Weatherby's class dealing with the origin of the devil's scepter shows me that you are opened minded, and that's a good start. What I'm all about here is attempting to get serious academics, like Henry, to just open their minds to the possibility that there is more at work in the universe than what we can see, hear, taste, smell, and touch," Doctor Kole explained.

"I can attest to that from my own personal experience," added Henry Weatherby. "And what I have seen is not only enlightening but frightening."

"Frightening only until we study and begin to understand it," insisted Kole. "Remember, things like the Aurora Borealis, or gun powder, was frightening to ancient peoples."

"Gun powder still scares the heck out of me," chuckled Henry.

"We are just starting to get serious scientists to not just 'poopoo' the supernatural, but to really take a look into it," moaned Doctor Kole.

"How did you get interested in it?" wondered Patterson.

A strange look swept across Doctor Kole's face. He suddenly looked saddened and scared as his eyes began to fill with tears.

"I was 10 years old," Kole began, obviously choking back tears. "I'll never forget it. It was late in the day, December 1st, 1958. I had taken my time on my way home from school, just like thousands of other children that day in Chicago. There was a slight dusting of snow on the ground, and we were all excited about Christmas coming. It was cold outside, so I supposed that the cold got the better of me, and I went inside to watch some television. I don't remember what time it was. It was still light out, but just barely. The sun set earlier at that time of year. When I walked into the house my mother was standing in front of the television. She was clutching the crucifix that she wore around her neck, crying and praying. I was stunned! I sat down in front of the television. I soon became aware of a horrible fire in a catholic school."

"The *Our Lady of the Angels* school fire," moaned Henry. "I remember it all too well."

"Every school kid in the city was traumatized by it. I was ten years old, and I never felt safe in school again. I found myself constantly thinking about how I would escape if it happened in my school," Kole sighed.

Henry nodded, "I did the same thing. Ninety-two children and three adults died."

"You had some sort of premonition?" pleaded Patterson.

Doctor Kole shook his head, "No. When my father got home from work that night, I heard him telling my mother that several nights earlier he'd had a dream that he was somewhere high up, and he was looking over the city. He looked to the west, and he could see a cloud of smoke and some kind of spire sticking up through the smoke. Right next to that spire he saw fire. About the time that the fire was burning, my father was working on a high tower where he works. It was about three and a half miles from *Our Lady of the Angels*. He looked in that direction and saw exactly what he had seen in his dream. He began to cry. I remember him saying to my mother that he wondered if God had shown it to him so he could warn them. She replied that no one would have believed him anyway. That incident had such a profound effect on me that it shaped my entire academic career."

"I can understand why," consoled Henry. "Did you ever speak to him about it?"

Kole nodded, "He told me the story when I began studying paranormal occurrences. He said that he was happy that I was doing what I was doing. He said that it was time that people started to take things like that seriously. He believed that it could save lives. He never forgot it and he never forgave himself for not trying to do something about it. I agreed with my mother. At that time, no one would have believed him until after it actually happened, and then they would have accused him of having something to do with it!"

"At that time, you were absolutely correct about how his report would have been received," agreed Henry. "Did he ever have any other episodes?"

Kole shook his head, "Not that he ever told me about."

Patterson was astounded, "That's incredible!"

"In my studies, I've found many such accounts," assured Doctor Kole. "As a matter of fact, since I've been teaching here, I've had a dozen students tell me about parents or relatives that had premonitions concerning that fire. It's my belief that that may have been the most psychically charged incident in Chicago's history. One of my students once told me that his older cousin told him that she was a student at that school when it happened. She was in one of the rooms on the first floor that evacuated at the first sign of smoke. She told him that she had often dreamed of walking through smoke filled halls in that building."

"Scary stuff," sighed Henry Weatherby.

"Are you psychic, Doctor Kole?" Patterson couldn't help but ask.

Kole grinned, "I have never had a dream come true. I have never had a correct premonition. And my wife and I do embarrassingly poorly with the Zener cards. I would say a resounding 'no', I am not psychic."

Chapter Three

Understanding

It had been a strange story, and it took Doctor Kole a few seconds to regain his composure.

"If this psychic is a fake, and that's the assumption that we have to work under, he's not going to let me or anyone in my community anywhere near him. He's probably already planted the seeds of cynicism in your aunt's mind against anyone who would challenge his abilities. He's warned her against those who would seek to discredit him. You need to understand how it works and how he is abusing it," Kole informed.

Once again Patterson nodded.

"First of all, what we're talking about here is extrasensory perception. The serious study of ESP began in the 1930s, at Duke University in North Carolina, J. B. Rhine and his wife Louisa Rhine where the first to conduct investigations into extrasensory perception. Louisa Rhine collected accounts of spontaneous cases. J. B. Rhine focused primarily on laboratory experiments. He relied on the use of a simple set of cards called Zener cards. These bare five symbols of a circle, a square, some wavy lines, a cross, and a star. There are five of each type of card in a pack of 25. In a telepathy experiment, the "sender" looks at each card for several seconds, in a different room, and a "receiver" guesses the symbols. In the case of clairvoyance or precognition, the pack of cards is hidden from everyone while the receiver tries to guess the order of the cards. This simple experiment has come under constant criticism from those intent on calling us pseudoscientists. However, I've had my students do this as a home lab assignment. I have them find two strangers to act as sender and receiver, then a couple that has been together for around five years, and lastly a couple that has been married for twenty or so years. It has been very revealing.

Statistical probability tells us that 79% of all people will get between 3 to seven out of twenty-five correct. And this is what my students find is true of the two strangers.

The probability of guessing 8 or more out of twenty-five correctly is 10.9%. However, my students find that as many as 25% of those that have been together for five years or longer can do this regularly. And with those married twenty years or more, this number rises to as much as 35%. With some couples married this long, guessing correctly can be as high as fifteen out of the twenty-five. Statistically the chances of getting 15 correct is about 1 in 90,000. Now I've never seen anyone get 20 out of 25, which has a probability of about 1 in 5 billion. However, what my students have indicated, is that telepathy may very well be familiar. Those who have spent a lot of time together are tuned into each other. And this won't surprise anyone who's been around people who have been married for many years."

"Has anyone ever guessed all twenty-five?" asked Patterson.

Doctor Kole chuckled, "I am still waiting for that! The statistical probability of that happening is about 1 in 300 quadrillion."

"But what you are saying is that people do tend to read each other's minds," marveled Professor Weatherby.

Doctor Kole nodded, "Yes, if they're married long enough. At any rate, in the 1960's parapsychologists became increasingly interested in the cognitive components of ESP, the subjective experience involved in making ESP responses, and the role of ESP in psychological life. A host of neuroscientists quickly jumped on board, and this was the beginning of true serious studies.

Because of this research, we now believe that there are nine different types of extrasensory perception.

The most popular form of extrasensory perception is clairvoyance. Clairvoyance is the ability to see beyond the earthly world. Some clairvoyants see visions of the past, present, or future in their mind, like a TV show or movies. Seeing the past is called postcognition, while seeing visions or images of the future is called precognition. Commonly they say that they receive these visual messages through their "third eye." The third eye is the gate or portal in the forehead that leads to a higher spiritual plane of enlightenment. Other clairvoyants see symbols, images, or auras, which surround us.

What my father may have had was a clairvoyant incident.

Clairaudience is related to clairvoyancy. Clairaudients have the ability to hear messages or receive information from sounds beyond our ordinary senses.

These messages may come from those that have passed beyond our life. They may come from the energies of the universe, a spirit, or animal messenger, or any other source that exists separate from our physical existence here on Earth.

Most often, these sounds are voices, reaching out with warnings or advice. Other times, a clairaudient might hear music, nature sounds such as birds chirping, or rhythms. Sometimes it may be akin to white noise or static, or even an internal dialogue. Mediums tend to fall into this group, although they represent a different type of ESP ability than those with clairvoyance or precognition. And, while mediums may be psychics, psychics are not always mediums.

Mediums are those who speak with the spirits of those who have passed on. They use trances to communicate with the energy of those that have transitioned from life to the beyond.

As with all psychic abilities, each medium works slightly differently. They fine tune their paranormal talents in their own way. Some mediums can only connect with their spirit guides, while others can communicate with anyone's spiritual energy. Some talents can build a bridge with both.

The third form of ESP is, psychometry, also called psychoscopy, which uses token object reading.

People with a talent for psychometry can read the history of objects through the energetic vibrations stored in those objects. Token object reading is also a form of divination. It works best with metals, but these vibrations are stored in everything we touch.

When reading an object, the psychic holds it in their hand or presses it to their forehead. Emotions leave a tangible record behind. Some people can even perceive the object's owner, experience sequences of their life, and grasp that person's personality.

Fourth is precognition. Those with precognition can divine events and experiences about locations or people that have yet to occur. In simple terms, precognition is the sixth sense to see into the future. This usually happens in dreams. Once again, it's not clear to me, but my father might have had a precognitive event.

The fifth type of ESP has often been called upon by agencies that include the U.S. Government, the Central Intelligence Agency, and local police agencies. All have tapped into the talents of remote viewers to help find missing persons, solving crimes, or gain insight into events. Remote viewing is also known as anomalous cognition, or second sight. Remote viewers project their minds to a distant locale and describe details of their target.

Some people have retrocognition, which is the sixth form of ESP. They have the ability to see into the past. Often connected to the sense of déjà vu, retrocognition is the opposite of precognition. Sometimes the psychic picks up information about a person's past, while other times, their knowledge relates to distant histories.

The seventh form of ESP is the one that everybody seems to believe in, to some extent. Telepathy is the ability to read people's minds or communicate with others without speaking.

You're probably familiar with the phenomenon of saying the same thing at the same time as another person or thinking of someone and getting a call from that person at that moment. These may very well be instances of telepathy at work. Telepathy can pick up on thoughts, emotions, and physical needs or desires. It can occur during waking moments, as well as in dreams. The Zener cards that I mentioned earlier are tools commonly used for testing telepathy. And, as I said, there are real indications that telepathy is familiar, not only between those who have developed it by spending time together, but also between those within a family.

The eighth and nineth form of ESP are the ability to move distant objects through non-physical means. Psychokinesis is actually an umbrella term for manipulating matter with the mind, which would include telekinesis. Telekinesis has come to generally refer to the movement of, or bending of objects, from a distance, whereas psychokinesis actually means 'soul movement', and now is most often used to refer to such phenomena as levitation and psychic healing."

"It would appear to me that there is a lot of overlap between these various forms of ESP," commented Professor Weatherby.

"Indeed, there are. And to complicate matters even more, many psychics exhibit more than one form, while some exhibit only one. Some seem to have control over them, and others have absolutely no control at all," chuckled Doctor Kole.

"Ok," sighed Patterson. "I think that I understand most of this, but how's any of this supposed to help my aunt?"

"I actually can't answer that," confessed Doctor Kole. "But you will need to get close to her and to her psychic friend and look for inconsistencies. Try to get your aunt to educate herself in the science of ESP. If the psychic is fake, he'll do his best to discourage this. That in itself might be enough to raise some suspicion for your aunt. It would also be of help to have someone like Doctor Weatherby's niece check the guy out. The Clarks have become good with these kinds of cases."

Patterson thanked Doctor Kole and he and Professor Weatherby left.

"Would you like me to talk to my niece about helping you?" offered Henry.

Patterson thanked Henry for his offer but confessed that he'd already spoken to Nora about having Duck and Jackie look into it. Henry wished his student good luck with the situation, shook hands, and went his own way. Patterson returned to the student parking lot. He was not as energized about his confronting the psychic as he had been that morning, but he was far from giving up. He got into his car and decided to drive to Nora's house.

While he drove, he mulled over what he'd learned from Doctor Kole. Professor

Weatherby was right, it was enlightening and frightening. It was especially alarming that there might be some truth to all of this nonsense. In fact, Patterson had zeroed in on the story that Doctor Kole had related when asked how he had gotten started in his field. The story of his father's dream was chilling and made Patterson terrified that some of his own nightmares could turn out to be premonitions of things to unfold in the future. A chill ran down his spine.

Chapter Four

In the Arms of One You Love

When Patterson got to Nora's house, they decided to spend the rest of the day at the lakefront. As usual, Patterson was quiet while he drove. Nora had gotten used to this and did most of the talking anyway. Once they got to Montrose harbor, Patterson parked. They grabbed a hotdog at the concession stand near where the boats were kept tied up. Nora remembered that on an earlier date, Patterson had taken her to a spot, not far from here, where one of the Monday Morning Murderer's victims had been found. She sincerely hoped that there would be no repeat of that incident. There wasn't. Patterson led Nora to the large square cut boulders which lined the shore at this part of Lincoln Park. They were like giant steps leading down to the water. The two sat on the highest level of the descending "steps". There was a beautiful view looking out over the lake to the southwest toward the loop from this spot. Patterson put his arm around Nora's waist and began to tell her about what he had learned from Doctor Kole. He especially told her about how he felt concerning his new view of dreams. Nora could sense his discomfort.

"You know, what he's talking about has got to be really rare. I mean, has anything that you've ever dreamed really come true?" Nora asked.

Patterson shrugged, "No, not that I can remember."

"And you have no idea how many times Doctor Kole's father had other dreams that he ignored or never put together with real events," Nora persisted.

"That's true," Patterson admitted.

"Everyone has had bad dreams," Nora sighed as she hugged Patterson. "And everyone has good dreams. I think that we should concentrate on the good ones. I think that if it's God's intent to give us information about something, then He would give us a way to use that information."

"Maybe it's not God," posed Patterson as he held Nora.

"The devil?" Nora sighed. "I don't think that the devil would take any chances that his plans would get screwed up by some human."

Patterson snickered, "I guess that you're right."

Maybe it was her logic or her kisses, but Nora was making Patterson feel better. It was nice to have someone that you loved. Perhaps this is what had been missing from Patterson's whole life. Suddenly Patterson realized how very devastating it must be for his Aunt Mariah to have lost the one that she loved. He instantly understood why she was so willing, even eager, to fall for this psychic who told her that he could communicate with Uncle Ted. Patterson almost wished that it could be true. There was comfort in the arms of someone that you love. He hated the con artist who was taking advantage of that feeling. More than ever, he needed to help his aunt. He couldn't help but think about Doctor Kole having mentioned having the Clarks help him with this matter. He really didn't want to press Nora, especially at this moment, but he just couldn't get it off his mind.

"Did you…." Patterson began, but then stopped, trying not to let his compulsion get the better of him.

"Did I what?" wondered Nora.

"Never mind," whispered Patterson.

Nora's hug loosened slightly, "Did I what?"

Patterson was sorry that he'd begun the question, as he knew that Nora wouldn't let it go now, and that when he did finish what he was about to ask, she would be mad at him.

"Never mind," Patterson sighed softly. "It's really not important."

"Did I talk to Jackie and Duck?" articulated Nora angrily.

"No" exclaimed Patterson, lying. "That's not what I was thinking!"

"Then what were you thinking?" demanded Nora sternly.

Patterson fumbled around trying to come up with something else quickly, "Did you…did you?"

Nora leaned away from the stuttering Patterson, "Come on spit it out. Did I what?"

Patterson couldn't think of anything else to say, so he said something almost as bad as what he had originally started to voice.

"Did you take your birth control pill today?" Patterson stammered stupidly.

Nora looked at him in disbelief.

"What?!" she bellowed loudly. "Is that all you think about? Is that all you think about? You would have been better off asking me if I'd talked to Jackie and Duck today! You are such a jerk!"

"I am so sorry," pleaded Patterson. "I didn't…"

"Yes, I took the stupid pill! Not that it's going to do you any good!" snapped Nora.

Patterson didn't know what to say or do as Nora stood up and stormed off in the direction of the car. At first Patterson was worried that she'd leave without him, but then he remembered that they had taken his car and that he had the keys in his pocket. He quickly felt his right pants pocket to verify that fact. Yes, they were there. She hadn't somehow picked his pocket. Patterson quickly considered the fix that he had gotten himself into. Should he rush after her or should he let her cool off first? There was no right answer. For the first time in his life, he wished that he were psychic. Would that ever come in handy in dealing with girlfriends!

Patterson just sat by himself on the huge rock facing out at the lake. He felt like such a fool. He hoped that Nora would come back. He worried that she would try to hitch a ride from someone. That could be dangerous. He would never forgive himself if anything bad ever happened to Nora. As Patterson sat looking out at the beautiful, romantic view, he realized that it was getting dark. He had to go after Nora, he had no choice. He headed back in the direction of his car. He really expected to see Nora either leaning against his car or sitting on its hood. She wasn't there. Now he would have to go looking for her. Patterson stood on the walkway where the boats tied up and considered his options. To his left, the sidewalk went on for a few hundred yards and then was cut off by the channel which the boats used to sail out from the basin onto lake Michigan. The only other thing in that direction was a stand of trees. To the right, the sidewalk wound around the harbor basin and eventually worked its way through the park to the city and public transportation. This would have been the logical, sensible way for someone to storm off in a fit of anger. Patterson thought about it for a second and started off in that direction, but then stopped and went the other way. Nora was not a logical, sensible person.

Patterson followed the sidewalk to its end at the water, then turned into the stand of trees. It didn't take long before he found Nora leaning against a tree.

"I'm sorry," Patterson pleaded, taking Nora's hands in his. "I'm an idiot. You know that about me."

Nora turned her eyes up from the ground to meet Patterson's.

"Sometimes…" Nora moaned.

"Not just sometimes," lamented Patterson. "But most of the time."

Nora couldn't help herself, she giggled.

"I know it, and I can't help myself," Patterson sighed. "I'm trying and trying, but I just can't help myself. I am an idiot."

"You certainly are," snickered Nora.

"Forgive me?" moaned Patterson.

Nora gazed at Patterson for a few moments, as if thinking about it.

"Ok, I forgive you, Snot," she groaned.

Patterson smiled, "Thank you."

Nora smiled back, "And to answer the question that you had really intended to ask, yes, I talked to Jackie and Duck. I told them all about your Aunt Mariah and they agreed to help."

Patterson grinned broadly, "They're better friends than I deserve."

"They're not your friends, they're mine," reminded Nora.

"And you deserve good friends. And I certainly don't deserve you," admitted Patterson as he leaned forward to kiss Nora.

"No, you don't deserve me," agreed Nora as she kissed him.

Chapter Five

Without Help

It was 1:38 p.m., Thursday afternoon August 21st, when Patterson arrived at the offices of Clark investigations. Nora worked the early shift starting at 8:30 in the morning, while her Aunt Alice worked the evenings. Phillip was getting coffee and his tenth doughnut of the day as Patterson awkwardly walked up to Nora's desk, wanting to kiss her 'hello,' but feeling out of place where she worked.

"Go ahead and kiss her, Son," Phillip snickered. "That seems to be what we do around here these days."

Patterson smiled and kissed Nora.

"So, your Nora's Doctor Strange?" chuckled Phillip.

"I don't have a doctorate yet, Sir," laughed Patterson.

"Good answer, Son," returned Phillip. "You can take her to lunch now if you want, I can hold down the fort."

"Actually, we're waiting for Jackie and Duck," informed Nora.

Phillip smiled, "That's nice. I'm happy to see all of you getting along so well."

With that Phillip returned to his private office.

"I'm sorry about the Doctor Strange crack from my boss," Nora apologized.

Patterson shrugged, "I deserve it, especially after what I did with the police. In fact, I'm surprised that he talked to me at all. And I have to admit that sometimes I do act kind of strange."

"Sometimes?" snickered Nora.

At that moment Jackie and Duck arrived at work. The three had planned to discuss Patterson's dilemma with his aunt over lunch that day. Nora buzzed Phillip and told him that they were leaving. He told them to have a good time and not to worry about coming back to the office, Alice would soon be in. The two couples walked across the street and down Broadway to the Golden Phoenix Chinese restaurant. They ordered the four person early bird dinner special. Patterson said that the lunch would be on him, as it was the least that he could do in return for their kindness.

"I honestly don't know why the two of you are willing to do this for me," offered Patterson. "I know that I'm a hard pill to swallow."

"Why not, after all, we all went to the same high school. That gives us something in common," returned Jackie.

"And, we've been chomping at the bit to try doing some investigating with no help from the people that we work with," added Duck.

"Well, I was really a jerk back in high school, and I guess that I haven't improved much with age," continued Patterson.

"We were all jerks in high school," interceded Duck. "Look at me! I thought that I was so cool back in high school. Then I met Mr. Clark and Professor Attlee and realized that I was just a bumbling fool. They really redefined 'cool' for me. I mean Professor Attlee was the fencing champion of his conference in college. How cool is that! And the guy knows everything. It's no wonder that a righteous babe like his wife fell in love with him."

Jackie glowered at Duck, "I don't know who Duck loves more, Phyllis or Professor Attlee."

Nora and Patterson chuckled.

Duck went on, ignoring Jackie's comment, "And look at Mr. Clark! The guy's Sam Spade and Phillip Marlow all rolled up into one. You don't get any cooler than Phillip Clark!"

When we're done here, I'll take you over to the headquarters of the bunko squad," Jackie explained. "You can go over their books of mugshots until you find the guy."

"The cops will let you do that?" asked Patterson.

Jackie nodded, "It's pretty much standard. It's about the only thing that most agencies have their apprentices do."

"We're lucky, the Clarks partner us with real licensed people to work real cases," Duck interjected.

"What if I don't find him?" wondered Patterson.

"You'll find him alright," returned Jackie. "And then I'll pull his rap sheet and check him for all known associates. Those guys usually have a whole army of informants working for them."

"If it's any help, his name is Yancy Gates," offered Patterson.

"It's probably an alias. Those guys change names more often than I change underwear," sighed Duck.

"That's not a pretty picture," snickered Jackie.

Everyone chuckled.

"What if this guy's on the level?" sighed Patterson. "After all, Aunt Mariah says that he hasn't asked her for any money. According to Doctor Kole at the university, the fakes always ask for money."

"The fakes always get money, or something valuable," corrected Jackie. "The good con men never have to ask for anything. Their marks just give it to them."

"They admire something that the mark owns," added Duck. "They never ask for it. They say things like, 'that's just like the one my grandmother had. I miss her so much'. Eventually the mark feels sorry for them and gives it to them. Most of the time the mark doesn't even know how valuable the thing is."

"Or, worse, the guy gets his mark to fall in love and marry him," appended Jackie. "Then, after he drains the bank accounts, he files for divorce and forces the sale of the home to get half of that."

"And that's not the worst case scenario," lamented Duck. "Sometimes the mark just has some kind of fatal accident."

Patterson looked truly distressed, "I hadn't even thought about anything like that."

"In our business we hear about stuff like that all the time," moaned Jackie.

"But, what if the guy's real?" Nora reiterated.

"That's pretty slim, but if he is, you'll have to reevaluate your objections," sighed Jackie. "It just might be that your aunt will be happier because of him."

Patterson nodded, "I suppose it's a possibility."

"You can cross that bridge when we come to it, if we come to it," proposed Duck. "But for right now, I think that we should eat our egg drop soup."

"If there is anything that I can ever do for the two of you, please, just ask," Patterson tendered.

"Yeah, when you inherit all your old man's money you can buy me a Maserati," Duck returned laughing. "On second thought, I'd never be able to afford the insurance on it."

After dinner Jackie and Duck drove Patterson and Nora the two and four tenths' miles north to the Rodgers Park police station, where northside bunco was headquartered. After showing their state licenses, Jackie and Duck escorted Nora and Patterson to a viewing room. There they perused several large, thick books, containing hundreds of photographs of persons who'd been arrested for various kinds of fraud. After an hour and three-quarters, Patterson perked with excitement.

"That's him!" exclaimed Patterson.

The name under the picture said Richard Gordon. Under the large bold letters was a list of aliases that Richard Gordon was known to use. Yancy Gates was not one of them, although Peter Yancy was listed.

Jackie went to the records office and filled out a form requesting the file on Richard Gordon. Then everyone sat down for what felt like an eternity.

"Does it always take this long to get a file?" asked Patterson.

Jackie shook her head, "Because we're P I's we're the lowest priority here."

"We would have had it in minutes if we'd gone to Captain O'Malley's precinct," sighed Duck.

"Yep, but tomorrow everyone at Clark Investigations would know about us asking for it," advised Jackie. "And I'd really like to keep this to ourselves for now."

"I hope this isn't going to get the two of you into any trouble," sighed Patterson.

Duck shook his head, "Not really, we just want to do this by ourselves."

"If we get in over our heads, we'll tell Professor Attlee or Phyllis," Jackie informed him.

"I'm sure that even Dave would give us a hand if we asked," suggested Duck.

"If you want an old school detective, it's sure Dave," chuckled Jackie. "I love working with him."

"I always feel like I'm in some old movie," laughed Duck.

"He scares me!" interjected Nora.

"That's just part of his persona," snickered Duck.

Finally, their number was called, and they were handed an invoice to pay for the search and the copies that were made. Jackie paid the bill and then gave one copy of the receipt to the clerk. The clerk rechecked her license and the receipt before handing over the copics of the file.

"Let me pay for that," insisted Patterson.

"Don't worry, we'll put it on your tab," laughed Jackie.

Patterson chuckled.

"Don't laugh, she's serious," Nora snickered.

The four left the police station and drove back to the Uptown Building.

"Now what?" asked Patterson as they drove.

"Now Duck and I study this file to see how this guy operates. Then we try to find a way to trip him up," informed Jackie.

"Couldn't I just show this file to my aunt?" Patterson asked.

"She'd only say that you made it up," Duck answered.

Jackie added, "Her boyfriend has most likely warned her that her family is going to try to fool her into believing that he's a con artist. The best thing that you can do at this point is absolutely nothing. Don't object to their relationship, don't even spend any time with them. The last thing that you want to do is make the guy feel that anyone's onto him. You don't want to make him feel uncomfortable. That could force his hand."

"Force his hand?" wondered Patterson.

"He's invested a lot of time and money in your aunt as a mark," returned Duck. "He wants his payoff."

"Invested money?" questioned Patterson.

"He's wined and dined her, and he's paid his people to gather information for him," answered Duck.

"He's not about to back off now," cautioned Jackie.

"I don't understand, what could he do?" considered Patterson.

Duck huffed, "They could run off and get married without telling anyone."

Jackie nodded, "So, it's best to just lay back and keep an eye on your aunt, but don't let them know that you're doing it. Remember, right now she's on his side. We're the enemy, and he's the one who's saving her from her inconsiderate family."

"It's a lot like working a person who's become abducted by a cult," groaned Duck.

"Just keep an eye on her to make sure that she's not about to bolt and let us do the rest," insisted Jackie.

"Believe it or not, we do know what we're doing," asserted Duck.

They had reached Patterson's car. They all said good night and left for their respective homes.

Chapter Six

The Great Mesmer?

It was 81 degrees at 10:00 a.m., Friday morning, although the humidity was only 69 percent, down from the 81 percent that it had been the day before, when Yancy Gates arrived at Mariah Emmerson's home on Winnetka's stately shoreline. Stanton, the butler, let Gates in, informing him that Mrs. Emmerson was awaiting him in the solarium.

"Madam has had a particularly difficult night, Sir," Stanton advised.

Gates thanked Stanton and hurried to the solarium.

The solarium was more like a reading room than the typical conservatory or greenhouse. In fact, there were no plants in it at all, although the large windows filled the room with sunlight and looked out over the lake. It was a beautiful room.

"This was Theodore's favorite room in the house," Mariah Emmerson informed him as Gates entered.

Gates looked around the bright room, "I can see why, but all this light is not good for you, Mariah."

Mrs. Emmerson looked at Gates curiously, "My doctor says that I should get out in the daylight. He says that it will do me good."

"That's the same doctor who told your husband that he should exercise for an hour every day?" Gates asked.

Mrs. Emmerson frowned.

"Yes, that worked out well, didn't it?" sighed Gates. "You have to learn to be more discerning about who you listen to. There are so many charlatans out there, Mariah."

"So true, Yancy," Mrs. Emmerson sighed. "What would I do without you?"

"I'm sure that you would do just fine, but you don't have to. I'm here for you. That's why Theodore put me in contact with you," Gates said cheerfully.

"That is just like Theodore. He was always looking out for me, taking care of me. Even in death, he's still watching out for my welfare," Mrs. Emmerson began to sob.

"Theodore is a good man," agreed Gates.

Mrs. Emmerson nodded.

"Now, what's this that I hear about you having a difficult night last night?" asked Gates as he escorted Mrs. Emmerson into the darker library which adjoined the solarium.

"It's so lonely in this big house, especially at night. I can't help but think about Theodore and the wonderful life that we had together," lamented Mrs. Emmerson.

"And will have again one day," added Gates. "You will have an even better life, an everlasting life."

"I know, Yancy, but that doesn't help much right now," moaned Mrs. Emmerson.

"You need to clear your mind. You have nothing to be concerned over. You have plenty of money and good health. What more could you want?" advised Gates.

"Theodore!" breathed the depressed widow.

"And he is here, watching over you. Always remember that," cajoled Gates.

"I know that being aware of that should comfort me, however it's just not the same," wept the distraught woman.

"You need to empty your mind. Clear everything from your thoughts and focus on getting rest," Gates counselled. "Have you tried those breathing exercises that I taught you?"

Mrs. Emmerson exhaled in frustration, "I've tried them over and over."

"You know, I have explained that there is another way," Gates reminded.

"I don't know about hypnotism. It scares me," confessed Mrs. Emmerson.

Gates chuckled, "I understand completely. But the gentleman that I know is a respected therapist. And anyway, no hypnotist can make you do anything that you don't want to do. It's not like in the movies. Hypnotism is a respected science. All that it will do is to help you take control of your own mind. It can help you to learn how to relax and be calm. There's no hocus pocus, or anything creepy, eerie, or bizarre about it at all. Professor Corrothers doesn't look like Svengali or Rasputin, the mad monk. He looks, and acts, like any other mental health professional."

Mariah Emmerson thought about what Yancy Gates was saying. She hadn't had a full night's sleep in the two weeks since Theodore had died. She was at her wits end and had no better ideas. Her doctor had given her sleeping pills, but Yancy had cautioned her as to how easy it was to get addicted to things like that. As she mulled it over in her mind, she considered how helpful Yancy Gates had been since they met two days after the funeral. In the week and a half since that chance meeting, Yancy had become her rock and guiding light. She would do it! She would try hypnotism. Yancy was delighted with her decision and immediately telephoned his friend, Professor Corrothers. As luck would have it, the Professor was available that very afternoon.

It was nearly three in the afternoon when Professor Corrothers arrived at the Emmerson household. And Yancy was correct in his assumption that Corrothers looked nothing like the stereotypical stage hypnotist or magician. Professor Corrothers was a short, plump, jovial man, with black, horn rimmed glasses, and a crewcut. He was neither handsome nor ugly. In fact, he looked more like an insurance salesman than a Professor.

Yancy greeted the professor as one would greet a close and old friend. He then introduced Corrothers to Mrs. Emmerson.

Professor Corrothers grasped the widow's hand warmly and said how sorry he was for her loss. Mariah felt an instant fondness for the man. They all went into the drawing room and sat down.

Corrothers smiled warmly and sympathetically, "Before we begin, I'd like to tell you a little about what I do."

Mariah smiled and nodded, "I would like that."

"Because of how hypnotism is portrayed in popular culture, it is quite commonly misunderstood. As a result, many people tend to reject it as a serious course of treatment," Corrothers began. "When administered in a customized, personal way, hypnosis can focus the subject's attention in such a way as to allow them to receive suggestions that can alter their thoughts and behavior in a positive manner. Studies suggest that it has limited side effects and may very well help many people with insomnia and other sleeping disorders."

Mariah Emmerson nodded slightly, "That's what Yancy has been telling me, and that's why I've decided to try it."

Professor Corrothers smiled broadly, "Good for you. But before getting started with sleep therapy hypnosis, I think that it is important that you know the facts about what it is, how it works, its pros and cons, and ways to make the most of this type of therapy."

Once again Mariah nodded, "I appreciate that very much, Professor."

Professor Corrothers chuckled as he went on, "Of course, many people see hypnosis as a form of mind control. These worries about mind control are usually based on stage acts or TV programs that do not present what hypnosis really is. During hypnosis, a person is generally more open to suggestions, but they still maintain the ability to control their decisions. While some people, who are highly susceptible to hypnotism, may seem to be fully under the influence of a hypnotist, decades of research demonstrate that most of these people are just doing what they want to do. They would act in these ways ordinarily if it were socially acceptable. They are merely using hypnosis as an excuse to act in that manner. In fact, when hypnotized you are not actually asleep. Instead, the person remains awake, but their focus is fixed in a way that may make them seem to be in a trance. The truth is that hypnosis is a state of consciousness in which the subject is focused intensely on a particular idea or image. This reduces their peripheral awareness. This is why they look as though they are in a trance. During hypnosis, a person's brain activity changes. They gain a receptiveness to new ideas. Hypnotherapy conveys suggestions to the subject in order to positively influence their thoughts and actions."

"I think that I understand," offered Mariah Emmerson.

Professor Emmerson continued, "My goal today, using sleep hypnotherapy, is not to make you fall asleep during our session, but rather, I hope to change negative thoughts or habits related to your sleep, so that you will be able to sleep better once hypnotherapy has been completed. I will attempt to reduce your anxiety and depression, both of which are certainly at the root of your sleeping problems. And by encouraging relaxation and creating an opportunity to reorient thoughts and emotions, I am hopeful that I can place the suggestion to 'sleep deeper', which has been shown to promote increased slow-wave sleep, which is important for your health."

"Well, it all sounds wonderful to me, Professor," sighed Mariah.

Professor Corrothers smiled brightly once again, "I must warn you that while roughly 15% of people are highly receptive to hypnosis, about one-third of all people are completely resistant to hypnosis. Most likely you will fall somewhere between the extremes. Because of this, it may take several sessions to fully achieve our goal. And, of course, those things that Mr. Gates has already suggested to you are sound and should be continued."

Mariah chuckled, "I understand. When can we give it a whirl?"

Corrothers laughed, "We can start right now, if you like."

"Why not?" Mariah returned enthusiastically. "The way I see it, the sooner we start, the sooner I get a good night's sleep."

"I was hoping that you'd say that," returned Corrothers energetically. "First, we should move to a room where you are extremely comfortable. It's better if it can be made dark and quiet."

"Actually, I believe that the library would work perfectly," suggested Yancy.

"Yes, I love the library," agreed Mariah.

"And there is a chase lounge that Mrs. Emmerson can recline on," added Yancy.

"Then, I will yield to your recommendations," agreed Professor Corrothers.

The three moved to the library. Yancy pulled the heavy blackout drapes and Corrothers told Mariah to lay down on the chase lounge. She did as she was told. The room was almost completely dark. Corrothers extracted a small penlight and a crystal attached to a light chain from his shirt pocket. Corrothers held the crystal above Mariah's face and focused the thin beam from the penlight on it. The crystal now shown brightly with a rainbow of colors as Corrothers began to spin the crystal.

"I want you to concentrate all your attention on the crystal," whispered Corrothers softly in a gentle rhythmical voice, almost sounding like music. "There is nothing but the crystal. Gaze into its light and only its light. There is nothing but the light."

Mariah did exactly as she was being instructed. She was exhausted from the stress of her husband's sudden death and the sleepless nights which followed. She was prime for sleep.

"Now, I want you to take long, deep, slow breaths. Breath in and out very slowly, very deeply. In and out. In and out," Corrothers instructed in his lulling, velvety voice. "I want you to relax. Let yourself go. Start by relaxing your toes. You can feel them becoming loose and limp. Now, your feet."

Professor Corrothers continued his soft methodical progression of relaxation techniques for Mariah's entire body, constantly reminding her to breath deeply and that she was sleepy. Eventually Corrothers could see that Mariah was completely loose and relaxed.

"Do you feel relaxed, Mariah?" asked Corrothers in a soothing calm tone.

"Yes," sighed Mariah softly.

"You feel more relaxed than you have in weeks," cooed Corrothers.

Mariah nodded slightly, "Yes, I do."

"Do you want to forget all your concerns and sleep well tonight?" enquired Corrothers gently.

"Yes, I want to sleep," returned Mariah as if in a trance.

"You believe in God and heaven, don't you, Mariah?" probed Corrothers.

Mariah responded that she did.

"You believe Mr. Gates when he says that Theodore has told him that he is in heaven now?" queried Corrothers.

"Yes, I believe," returned Mariah.

"Theodore is safe and happy," pressed Corrothers warmly and softly.

"Yes, Theo is happy," replied Mariah.

"You know all this?" questioned Corrothers. "And still, you have trouble sleeping?"

"I miss Theo," sighed Mariah softly.

"You know that he is always with you. Love never dies. Theodore is always in your heart. Theodore is always watching over you," advised Corrothers soothingly.

"Theo is with me," Mariah repeated.

"Theodore is with you," affirmed Corrothers.

"He is with me," agreed Mariah.

"Theo has sent Yancy to help you and keep you safe," impressed Corrothers.

"Theo sent Yancy to me," reiterated Mariah.

"Yes, Theodore has sent Yancy to you. Theo has chosen Yancy to help you. Yancy will help you to sleep. Yancy will help you to feel better," implanted Corrothers.

"Yancy will help me," echoed Mariah.

"Yes, Yancy will help you," reinforced Corrothers. "And you will sleep soundly, and you will sleep deeply, this night, and every night thereafter."

"I will sleep soundly," parroted Mariah.

"You will have no further stress or anxiety. You will sleep, sleep deeply," reassured Corrothers.

"I will sleep deeply," repeated Mariah.

"How do you feel about sleeping now, Mariah?" asked Corrothers kindly.

"I feel good about sleep," Mariah confessed slowly and softly.

"How do you feel about your friend Yancy?" inquired Corrothers.

"Yancy is my friend, he was sent to me by Theo. Yancy will help me," professed Mariah.

"Yes, Yancy will help you. Yancy will help you to sleep and he will help you in every way," Corrothers suggested.

"Theo sent Yancy to help me," Mariah confirmed.

"Yes, Theodore sent Yancy," agreed Corrothers.

Mariah lay peacefully on the chase lounge breathing calmly.

"Now, when I count to three you will awake. You will keep all that we've done deep inside your subconscious. You will feel very well, at peace, and you will sleep soundly and deeply whenever you want to sleep," Corrothers suggested. "One, two, three!"

Mariah awoke.

"How do you feel?" asked Corrothers.

Mariah sat up, looking around her with slight confusion.

"I feel good. I feel very good, Professor,"
Mariah sighed quietly. "Did it work?"

"I feel that we made very good progress,"
Corrothers said happily. "However, we won't
really know until tonight. Remember not to
drink any coffee or alcohol before bed. Also,
don't do anything stimulating, like engage in
any sort of game, watch television, or exercise.
You might want to listen to soft, easy music,
and perhaps have a hot drink before bed. But
remember, not anything with caffeine or a lot of
sugar, or alcohol. I'm sure that Yancy will help
you."

"Oh, yes," sighed Mariah. "Yancy is such a
help to me."

"Now, please keep me informed of how you're
sleeping. We'll need to do several more
sessions," continued Corrothers.

"How much do I owe you, Professor?" inquired
Mariah.

"I can't accept any money until I know that I've
helped you. It just wouldn't be right,"
answered Corrothers.

"Theo always insisted that the workman is
worthy of his wages," insisted Mariah.

"In due time, dear lady," avowed Corrothers as he said goodbye and left.

Chapter Seven

Research

Duck and Jackie spent all the free time that they had pouring over the file that they had acquired the day before. At lunch time Jackie went over to the eighteenth precinct headquarters and pulled files on all the known associates of Richard Gordon. There were many, and most had a lengthy list of aliases. However, one popped out immediately, a Reverend Carlton A. Corrothers, Ph.D.!

According to Reverend Corrothers' file, he was the founder of the Church of Blessed Deliverance. He'd been investigated several times for suspected fraud in raising funds for a variety of sketchy charities, but never convicted of anything. His church, although nondenominational, was duly licensed in the State of Illinois. The 'good Reverend' had graduated from a quasi-religious institution in France and had been ordained by the same institution. Before his religious enlightenment, Carlton Corrothers had held many jobs in various areas of the theater, mostly as a bit part actor. Carlton Corrothers' only long term job was as a stage hypnotist in Atlantic City. Jackie was instantly interested in this fact. It seemed just the sort of thing that could be useful to Richard Gordon's scheme concerning Patterson's Aunt Mariah.

Upon returning to the Clark offices, Jackie was happy to see that Nora had replaced her Aunt Alice at the front desk. Jackie asked Nora if Patterson had mentioned anything about his aunt seeing a hypnotist. Nora couldn't recall that Patterson had ever mentioned anything about a hypnotist. But then, he might have, and she'd just forgotten. Jackie asked Nora to get in touch with Patterson as soon as she could in order to find out.

It was nearly six in the evening when Duck returned from tailing someone with Dave. Jackie informed him of what she had found out.

"So, has Yancy introduced Aunt Mariah to this guy yet?" wondered Duck.

Jackie shrugged, "Nora hasn't been able to get in touch with Patterson all day."

Duck scowled, "That guy is always underfoot, hanging around, getting in the way. Now, when you'd like to talk to him, he does a disappearing act."

"I just hope that he's not sticking his nose into our case!" declared Jackie.

"I don't know if we should have ever gotten involved with this guy," lamented Duck.

"If he's really on the level with us, his aunt could use our help," reminded Jackie.

Duck glowered, "If he's being on the level with us."

Jackie sighed.

The sun was starting to set at 7:43 p.m. when Patterson arrived at his Aunt Mariah's estate on the shore of Lake Michigan in Winnetka. It was 76 degrees with the wind wafting in off the lake at about seven miles per hour. It was cloudy, but Patterson didn't notice any of this as Stanton opened the door for him.

"How's my aunt?" Patterson asked hurriedly.

"She's feeling much better since she had her session with Professor Corrothers this afternoon, Sir," returned Stanton.

Patterson gazed at the butler quizzically, "Professor Corrothers?"

"One of Mr. Gates' acquaintances, I believe, Sir," offered Stanton.

"One of Mr. Gates' acquaintances?" reiterated Patterson.

Stanton nodded coldly, "Yes, Sir. I believe that he's some sort of hypnotist."

"Hypnotist!" exclaimed Patterson.

Stanton nodded, "Your aunt has been having difficulties sleeping."

Patterson stood in the foyer with Stanton for several seconds.

"What do you think of this Gates guy, Stanton?" inquired Patterson.

Stanton stood fidgeting uncomfortably, "It is not my place, Sir, to comment or voice an opinion on missus's companions."

Patterson considered Stanton carefully, "My uncle loved you, Stanton."

Stanton's eyes filled with tears, "And I, him, Sir. He was a good man."

"Indeed," returned Patterson. "What would you have told him about Yancy Gates?"

Stanton exhaled hard, "I would have told him that Mr. Gates, in my opinion, is a scoundrel. I don't know exactly what he is after, but I believe that his intentions are less than honorable."

"I agree. You have to help me keep an eye on my Aunt Mariah," pleaded Patterson.

"I'll gladly do whatever I can, Mr. Patterson," returned the butler.

"Is he here now?" asked Patterson.

Stanton shook his head, "He's gone home to get his belongings. He's staying the night."

Patterson looked disturbed as he asked Stanton to take him to his aunt.

Mariah Emmerson was finishing her dinner in the dining room. She was happy to see her nephew. She asked him why he'd come to see her. Patterson wanted to tell her that he was concerned about Yancy Gates but decided that she would only take his concern as meddling in her affairs, so he said that he was concerned as to how she was getting along in the big empty house.

Mariah smiled at her nephew and expressed that he was kind to be concerned about her. She invited him to join her in dessert. Patterson accepted. It would be the perfect opportunity to engage in small talk. He hoped that the conversation would turn to what he was studying in college, as he could lie and tell her that he was taking a class in paranormal psychology. He hoped that by doing this he could ease into talking about her relationship with Yancy Gates without the dialogue becoming confrontational. It worked.

"So, what has my nephew been up to this summer?" Mariah asked cordially.

Patterson smiled, "Actually I've been taking classes at the University of Chicago all summer."

His aunt seemed happy, "That's good, making good use of your time instead of frittering it away, smoking reefers, listening to that awful music, and protesting everything."

"I truly like school," confessed Patterson.

Once again Aunt Mariah smiled approvingly, "And what have you been studying?"

"This summer I took a class in the history of ancient religious artifacts taught by Professor Henry Weatherby, Ph.D.," Patterson disclosed.

"Doctor Weatherby!" exclaimed Aunt Mariah. "The fellow that wrote that book about the Devil's Scepter?"

Patterson chuckled, "Yes, that's the guy."

"That must have been so interesting," declared Aunt Mariah.

"It was very, but not half as interesting as the other class that I took. It was about parapsychology," Patterson returned.

A funny look came across Aunt Mariah's face.

"Parapsychology?" his aunt echoed. "You mean like psychics, mediums, and mind readers?"

"I know that you must think that I'm just being weird, creepy, dark, Patterson again, like when I was in high school. But, no, I haven't lost my mind. It's become a respected science," Patterson argued.

Aunt Mariah chuckled, "I don't think that you've lost your mind. I just wonder why a journalism major would take a class like that?"

"Actually, it was Uncle Ted who encouraged me. He told me that a journalist should have a multifaceted education so that he can have an open mind about the stories that he writes," Patterson submitted.

Aunt Mariah nodded, "Yes, Theo did believe that one should learn as many different things as one could."

"I tell you, Aunt Mariah, it's absolutely incredible," Patterson went on excitedly.

"I'm so glad that you think so," sighed Aunt Mariah. "The fact is that I have a friend that is a psychic. And as luck would have it, he's coming over tonight."

Patterson acted as if he were surprised, "I would so like to meet him."

Just then Stanton entered the room.

"Mr. Gates, madam," Stanton announced.

Yancy Gates was close on Stanton's heels.

Aunt Mariah laughed aloud, "You must be psychic, we were just talking about you."

Yancy Gates looked at the two with confusion.

Aunt Mariah explained that she and her nephew, Patterson, had been discussing a class that he had taken that summer. Gates listened closely.

"So, Mr. Steward," Gates addressed. "Are you a skeptic or a believer?"

Patterson smiled, "Very much a believer."

"Who taught the class that you took?" Gates asked as he sat down.

 "Doctor Stan Kole," replied Patterson. "Do you know him?"

Gates shook his head, "Only by reputation. I know that he's not actually psychic himself. I suppose that he taught you that most of us are charlatans."

"Quite the contrary," Patterson objected. "His father was one of the people that had a premonition about the *Our Lady of the Angels* school fire. Because of that he is reluctant to call anyone a fake."

Gates nodded his head, "That was an awful tragedy, and one of the most psychically charged events in history. People are still psychically interfacing with those who died in that horrible fire."

"I have to admit that it is scary that the idea that some of the things that I've dreamed might actually come to fruition," admitted Patterson.

"Most dreams are just dreams and nothing more," impressed Gatcs.

"I would love to hear all about what it's like to be a psychic?" Patterson pressed.

Gates frowned, "It's really not all that exciting. I'd rather not talk about it. Once people hear that I'm a psychic they forget that I'm also a person. It's all people want to talk about."

"You'll have to forgive my nephew, he's a journalism major in college and he just can't help himself," Aunt Mariah apologized.

Patterson chuckled, "My aunt is right. I'm just one question after another, sorry."

Gates smiled slightly, "Of course, you're forgiven."

"Actually, I have to be off anyway," Patterson sighed. "My girlfriend gets off of work at ten and she'll be expecting me."

With that Patterson arose, shook Gates' hand, kissed his aunt, and made his way to the front door. On his way out he encountered Stanton.

"As I said, keep me apprised of what's going on here," Patterson whispered to Stanton.

The butler nodded in agreement.

Chapter Eight

Dinner With the Boss

When Patterson arrived at the Uptown Bank Building it was just after Ten in the evening. Nora was just getting ready to leave when Patterson walked into the Clark offices.

"Where have you been all day?" Nora barked at Patterson. "I've been trying to get in touch with you!"

Patterson looked at his girlfriend sheepishly, "I've been thinking."

"Thinking!" bellowed Nora. "About what?"

Just then, hearing the discourse, Phillip walked out of his office.

"Leave the man alone," Phillip grumbled. "A man's gotta' think sometimes. There ain't nothing wrong with thinking."

The two looked at Phillip with guilty expressions on their faces.

"There's far too little thinking going on in this world these days, if you ask me," Phillip continued.

"Thank you, sir," asserted Patterson.

"So, still dating Doctor Strange I see?" Phillip asked Nora.

"Yes, Mr. Clark," Nora squeaked out.

Phillip looked at the college freshman carefully. Both Nora and Patterson felt as uncomfortable as they had ever been in their lives. The corner of Phillip's mouth turned up in a half smile as the old detective extended his right hand to Patterson. It took Patterson a moment to realize that Phillip was offering to shake his hand. Patterson grasped Phillip's hand solidly. He couldn't believe how strong of a grip the old detective had.

"I suppose that I should get used to you, if you're going to be hanging around here," Phillip chuckled.

"I'd like to apologize…" Patterson began, but Phillip cut him off.

"No reason to apologize, son. No harm was done, and it's all forgotten about," Phillip exonerated.

Patterson smiled, "Thank you, Sir."

"I gotta say it was ballsy of you, especially the part about saying that you had information from Pauli Boy," Phillip snickered. "That's the kind of stuff that can get you killed."

Patterson swallowed hard, "So I've been told, Sir."

Phillip chuckled, "What's your name? I don't want to keep calling you Doctor Strange, I think that it bothers Nora."

Patterson smiled, "It's Patterson Steward, Sir."

Phillip cringed, "Wow, I think that I like Doctor Strange, better. How about I call you Pat?"

"That's what most of my friends call me, Sir," informed Patterson.

"I hope that we can become friends," offered Phillip.

Patterson smiled.

Just then the door leading in from the hallway burst open and in hustled Jackie and Duck. The two were obviously surprised to see Phillip standing there shaking hands with Patterson. Phillip looked at the new arrivals.

"Well, it seems that the gang's all here," Phillip chuckled. "Have the four of you got plans for this evening?"

"No, Mr. Clark," answered Jackie.

"Nonsense," declared Phillip. "It's next to the last Friday night in August. Young people like you should be doing something on a night like this."

"Nope, no plans at all, Sir," stammered Duck.

Phillip chuckled, "How about I take the four of you out for pizza?"

"We couldn't, Sir," rejected Jackie.

"Why not?" Phillip pressed. "You just said that you got no plans. We could drive over to Gulliver's and spend some time getting to know each other. Maybe you can let me in on what the four of you got cooking that's such a big secret!"

The four looked at each other suspiciously.

"Come on, you don't think that I'm so old that I don't know what's going on right under my nose?" Phillip laughed. "Do you think that apprentices from Clark Investigations can have files pulled anywhere in this city without me finding out about it?"

"I'm sorry, Mr. Clark," sighed Jackie.

Phillip laughed heartily, "No need to be sorry, just let me in on what you're up to."

Jackie smiled, "Ok, thank you."

The five piled into three cars and drove the five and a quarter miles to Gulliver's on Howard Street.   They parked their cars on the Evanston side of Howard Street and crossed to Gulliver's.

"I used to come here every Friday night with Phyllis when she was little and then we came every Friday night with Ben once he moved here from California," Phillip reminisced as they waited to be seated. "But, now that they're married, they got better things to do."

"I don't think that they have better things to do, just different things," Duck consoled.

Phillip laughed loudly, "Yes, better things, you better believe it, Son. What's wrong with this boyfriend of yours, Jackie?"

"You'll have to excuse him, he's just an idiot," Jackie snickered. "He never thinks before he talks."

Duck looked defiant, "What could they be doing that's better than having a night out with your grandfather?"

Phillip continued to laugh, "I don't know about the young men of today."

Duck looked at them with confusion.

Jackie shook her head, "Think about it, Duck! They are two, young, married people!"

"Oh! I didn't think of that," Duck admitted with embarrassment.

"When I was your age, that's all that I thought about," Phillip chuckled as he slapped Duck on the back.

The five were finally seated and ordered.

"Now, who's gonna fill me in on what's going on?" insisted Phillip.

"Maybe it would be best if Patterson laid it all out for you, Mr. Clark," conceded Jackie. "It concerns his aunt."

Phillip looked at Patterson, "Well, go ahead, spill it, Kiddo."

Patterson looked nervous and scared as he began the story about his Aunt Mariah and Yancy Gates. Phillip listened intently. When Patterson finished his explanation, Phillip turned to Jackie.

"So, what have the two of you dug up?" Phillip asked.

Jackie told her boss about Gates' record and real name. She also added that Gates had an associate who was a hypnotist.

"And that's why I was trying to get ahold of you all day," Nora interrupted. "They wanted to know if that guy Gates has introduced your aunt to a hypnotist."

Everyone turned to Patterson.

"In fact, Stanton, her butler, told me that Gates brought around a hypnotist this afternoon. Aunt Mariah had some sort of treatment to help her sleep," Patterson divulged.

Everyone turned to Phillip. Phillip rubbed his chin and thought. Several minutes of silence passed.

"You were right to be concerned about this guy," Phillip said slowly. "Widows are easy prey for good grifters, and this guy sounds good."

"Do you think that Gates' hypnotist friend can hypnotize Patterson's aunt into giving him all her money, or anything like that?" asked Duck.

Phillip shook his head, "You guys did a good job as far as you've gone. No, you can't hypnotize anyone into doing anything that they wouldn't do or want to do anyway. I don't think that your aunt is the kind of person that would just hand over her money to anybody."

"That does not sound like my aunt, no matter how bad she feels about losing Uncle Ted. No, she's not the type to give anything away," Patterson insisted.

"You did say that this hypnotist guy was also some sort of Reverend?" Phillip asked Jackie.

Jackie nodded, "It sounds like some kind of bogus church if you ask me."

Phillip snickered, "Of course it is. What kind of preacher hangs out with guys like Gates? But these phony ministers can be pretty convincing. Do you think that he could convince your aunt to donate or fund some kind of crazy charity?"

Once again Patterson shook his head, "My aunt believes in God and Jesus, but she really is not church minded at all. She wouldn't give money to any church, even if the Pope himself told her to."

"Ok, so we don't have to worry about that," Phillip said with relief. "The hypnotist preacher can't get her to do anything that she isn't inclined to do on her own, however, between the two of them, they could get your aunt to marry Gates."

"My Aunt Mariah loved Uncle Ted very much. I don't think that she could fall for someone so soon after his death," denounced Patterson.

Phillip shook his head, "Not under normal circumstances, but this Gates guy has probably told her that Ted is the one that has sent him to her. She trusts the guy and now he's wining and dining her. He's helping her. He's found her a therapist to help her sleep. She's developing a soft spot in her heart for this guy. Now enter the phony preacher hypnotist and he gives her hypnotic suggestions that Gates is a good guy. Gates is looking out for her. She should trust Gates. All of these things are things that, deep down, she really wants to do. Once they get her feeling really comfortable with her relationship with Gates, then it ain't that much of a leap to matrimony."

"Wow!" exclaimed Duck, "That makes it sound so simple."

Phillip sneered, "It is simple, and it happens all the time. The only thing that you've got on your side is that it takes time to achieve."

"What can we do about it?" asked Patterson.

"What you can't do is confront her with all this. These guys have already cautioned her to not believe her family when the family says terrible things about them. They've probably told her that her family is after her money. They might even be doing that in her hypnosis sessions. No, you've got to figure out a way for her to find out for herself that these guys are con-men," Phillip advised. "It might be best to casually slip in little antidotes about people you've heard of who've been swindled by con-men."

"How do we do that, Sir?" asked Jackie.

"You've just got to find a way," answered Phillip.

"Me?" sighed Jackie.

"You and Duck," Phillip smiled. "After all, it's your case."

Jackie and Duck looked at each other skeptically.

Phillip chuckled, "Don't worry, now that you've told me about it, you have a supervising licensed detective, so it's all legal."

Phillip turned to Patterson, "You got a buck on you, Kiddo?"

Patterson looked at Phillip oddly.

"From what I can deduce from the looks of you, you got plenty of bucks," Phillip chuckled.

Patterson nodded.

"Fork one over, Son," Phillip commanded.

Patterson did as he was told, and Phillip took the dollar.

"Thank you, now that we've received renumeration for the case, it's all copasetic," Phillip explained. "Now, let's eat our pizza!"

Chapter Nine

Days Off

Saturday, August 23rd, was a mostly cloudy day in Chicago. The temperature only reached eighty-two, with the humidity getting as high as 85% late in the day. Phyllis and Benjamin had gotten tickets to the Cubs' game from Phillip's booky, Morty. The Cubs were playing the New York Mets. It was the fifth from the last game of the season and the Cubs were 73 wins and 85 losses for the season, an exceptionally good season for the Cubs. They finished the season fifth in the National League East, seventeen games behind the Pittsburg Pirates.

"I don't know how Chicagoans get all worked up over the Cubs, they're pathetic," Benjamin complained as they made their way to the box seats that they had tickets for.

Phyllis looked at him disgustedly, "The Dodgers aren't a whole lot better."

"They're second in the west," objected Benjamin.

Phyllis laughed, "Yeah, twenty games behind the Cincinnati Reds. The Cubs are only seventeen games behind the Pirates."

"Doesn't matter, second is second and fifth is fifth," grumbled Benjamin. "Although I gotta admit, this is a great ballpark."

Phyllis smiled, "It sure is. Gramps and Uncle Sean used to take me here all the time when I was little."

"And then they'd take you to Mrs. Rice's under the Ravenswood 'L' for even more hotdogs, as if the half dozen that you'd eaten at the game wasn't enough," snickered Benjamin.

"We went to Mrs. Rice's for the *Green River* soda," protested Phyllis. "They never served *Green River* at the games."

"And tell me, swear on the bible, that you didn't have another hotdog with your *Green River*," implored Benjamin.

Phyllis giggled, "Well, it's just not the same without the hotdog. They were soooo good with the poppyseed bun and that gigantic slice of pickle!"

Benjamin laughed, "I know, they still are. How is it that you never got fat?"

"Clarks have a really high metabolism," Phyllis continued to giggle. "And you should be happy that we do, or else you'd be married to a cow."

Benjamin laughed, "What makes you think that I would have married Elsie, the Borden Cow?"

Phyllis snickered, "I always thought that it was my charm and intelligence that made you fall in love with me."

"I hate to say it, but that smoking hot body of yours didn't hurt," Benjamin laughed.

Phyllis frowned and playfully punched Benjamin's arm, "And here I thought that you weren't like other guys."

"The first thing that I noticed as you stepped off that train from Chicago was that you were as hot as a pistol, and not because of the temperature. In fact, you were so good looking that I almost couldn't speak!" Benjamin admitted.

"You don't have any trouble speaking any more, unfortunately," Phyllis snickered.

Benjamin looked at her uneasily, "I thought that you liked the fact that I'm smart?"

"Smart, not smartass," Phyllis corrected. "And you really don't have to always go on and on about every little detail of even the most insignificant historical event."

"All right," Benjamin said indignantly. "I don't have to go on and on. I don't have to say anything at all."

"You, not talk?" Phyllis laughed loudly.

"Just to prove it, I won't say another word until the seventh inning stretch," Benjamin pledged.

"You're on," agreed Phyllis.

The two settled down into their seats and the game began.

Benjamin looked over the official scorecard and roster as the first batter stepped up to the plate.

"Did you know…" Benjamin started but was cut off by Phyllis laughing.

"I knew it," Phyllis roared. "You didn't even make it through the first batter!"

Benjamin shut up, scrunched down in his seat, and sulked. The Cubs lost to the Mets 6 to 8, but the hotdogs were good.

As Phyllis and Benjamin suffered through another Cubs' disaster, Jackie and Duck spent the afternoon sailing on Patterson's boat with Patterson and Nora. Nora had packed a nice picnic lunch and they actually had an enjoyable time. After a while, the conversation ultimately turned to Patterson's Aunt Mariah and her relationship with Yancy Gates.

"I've been thinking about this all last night and today," confessed Jackie. "Do you think that you could setup a lunch or dinner with your aunt to meet your new girlfriend?"

Patterson nodded, "I'm sure that she would love to meet Nora."

"The problem is keeping Gates away," interjected Nora.

"I don't think that would be any problem at all," Patterson posed. "When I was there Friday, Gates came in and Aunt Mariah told him that I had taken a course at the University in parapsychology. He was noticeably disturbed. When I began asking him some rather innocuous questions about being a psychic, he replied that it wasn't all that interesting and declined to answer, saying that he hated that people saw him only as a psychic and not as a person. I figured that he really didn't want anyone that's studied parapsychology to be asking him any questions."

"You've studied parapsychology?" queried Nora.

"No, but I told Aunt Mariah that I'd taken a class this summer," snickered Patterson.

"That could have been dangerous if he'd started asking you any questions," scolded Jackie.

Patterson scowled, "I would never have done it except Doctor Weatherby took me over to meet Doctor Kole, the professor that actually teaches that class. We spent over an hour together. He gave me a quick rundown on what he taught."

"Man, you were still taking a chance," Duck sighed.

"I didn't have a choice, he just popped in while I was visiting Aunt Mariah," asserted Patterson. "She was the one who told him about me taking the class."

"Why did you tell her that in the first place?" complained Nora.

"I had hoped to drop some little seeds of doubt about the guy. I never expected him to be coming over for the night," moaned Patterson.

"Did you plant your seeds?" asked Jackie.

Patterson shook his head, "The bum showed up too soon."

"Ok, I don't think that it did us any harm," posed Duck. "And it may well have helped our cause. It's obvious that Gates is going to avoid Patterson and that's good."

"Why do you want me to introduce Nora to Aunt Mariah?" Patterson queried.

"You better believe that Mr. Clark is right about Gates getting your aunt primed for interference into their relationship by relatives. Anything that you might say is going to fall on deaf ears. On the other hand, Nora is not a relative. Presumably, she has no idea what is going on, and even if she did, why would she care?" Jackie expounded. "You can say that Nora is a secretary at some insurance company. She works in the fraud investigation division. Then Nora can talk about cases that she's had access to, cases where people have been swindled or even murdered by con-men or con women. The cases should not be exactly like her situation, but close enough to raise some suspicion."

"You're brilliant!" exclaimed Duck.

"That's what I've been telling you," chuckled Jackie.

"It really pays to hang around with Mrs. Attlee," Duck added.

"Maybe I'm brilliant, but you sure aren't. Phyllis had nothing to do with that idea," protested Jackie.

"What's wrong with learning from the person that you're working with?" Duck admonished. "I've learned loads from Professor Attlee and from Dave. That's what an apprentice is supposed to do."

"Obviously, they haven't taught you anything about how to treat your girlfriend," teased Patterson.

"You should talk," snickered Nora.

Jackie chuckled, "You mean that Duck isn't the only guy that's clueless around here?"

Nora laughed, "Are you kidding? The other day Pat started to ask me if I'd asked you and Duck for help. Then he realized that I'd be mad, so instead he asked me if I'd taken my birth control pill that day."

Jackie roared with laughter.

"Alright, I'm an idiot," Patterson declared.

When the sun set on Lake Michigan at 8:45 p.m., the four headed into the yacht club. It was a beautiful evening and the four decided to sit on the boat and watch the stars from Patterson's slip, but first Patterson went to the public phone on the shore end of the pier and called his aunt to setup dinner Sunday evening. She was thrilled and excited to be meeting her nephew's girlfriend.

At the Emerson house in Winnetka, Mariah informed Yancy that they would be having company for dinner the next evening. He wasn't excited or thrilled at all.

"Is this the young man that I met Friday night?" wondered Gates.

Aunt Mariah told him that it was. She also informed Gates that Patterson was the only member of her family that she had any use for at all.

"It's just that I feel like I'm being put under a microscope by people like him," Gates complained.

Mariah laughed, "He's just an inquisitive young college student. He has always been full of questions. I believe that is why Theo loved him so much.”

“It’s not him,” Gates pleaded. “It’s his whole generation. I don’t know what’s worse, people who think that I’m a fraud or people who believe in us and think that we can turn it on and off at will. But I do know that it’s people that have a little bit of book knowledge and think that they’re experts that are the most annoying.”

“I understand completely,” offered Mariah. “It must be hard on you, and I won’t feel hurt if you should decide not to be here for dinner tomorrow. After all, youngsters that age can be terribly trying. And I don’t even know this girl yet. Perhaps it would be best if you did do something else.”

“I would hate to hurt the feelings of someone important to you,” considered Gates.

“Oh, he won’t be hurt,” Mariah rejected. “He’s going to be much too busy trying to impress me with his new girlfriend.”

Gates chuckled and agreed.

Chapter Ten

Dining With Aunt Mariah

It was late afternoon when Patterson and Nora arrived at the Emmerson mansion in Winnetka. Stanton, the butler, opened the door for them, greeting them happily.

"Just so you know, Sir, Mr. Gates will not be dining with you today," Stanton informed.

Patterson smiled, "That is good news. It will make our mission much easier if he's not here to direct the conversation."

Stanton escorted the two through the cavernous house to the solarium where Patterson's Aunt Mariah was waiting for them. Mariah was genuinely happy to see the young couple. Patterson introduced Nora to his aunt and the three sat down in the room overlooking the lake. Stanton brought in a tray of cheese and crackers and a pitcher of lemonade.

"I am so happy to meet you, young lady," Aunt Mariah said cheerily. "I wondered when my nephew was going to find some nice young lady. How did the two of you meet?"

Nora smiled and thanked Mariah and began to explain their long relationship.

Nora began, "Actually, we first met in high school. Patterson and I were in the same grade."

"Shame on you Patterson," Mariah interrupted. "You've been dating this young lady since high school, and this is the first time that you've brought her around to meet me?"

"Oh, no!" corrected Nora. "We were only friends in high school."

Mariah chuckled, "Of course, he was so dark and strange back then that no girl would have ever dated him."

Patterson laughed and thanked his aunt sarcastically.

"Well, after we graduated, we lost contact for two years," Nora resumed. "But the first week of this July, we bumped into each other at the Art Institute. We spent the rest of the day together and at the end of the day we decided to meet again at Lincoln park zoo that Saturday. That's when he asked me to go see the Stones at the Chicago Stadium with him. Since then, it seems like we've been doing everything together."

Mariah smiled as she listened, "Oh that sounds so nice. I'm so happy for the two of you. Patterson never seemed to do very well with ladies. Frankly, I was starting to wonder about him."

"Again, thank you very much, Aunt Mariah!" Patterson interrupted. "You needn't be concerned about my sexuality. As you can see, Nora is very female."

Nora laughed, "And I can assure you, Aunt Mariah, Patterson is very interested in women."

Mariah snickered, "That is very good news. So, you say that you went to see stones at the Chicago Stadium on you first real date?"

Patterson laughed, "Not stones, the Rolling Stones. They're a rock band, a very popular one."

"At the hockey place?" wondered Mariah.

Patterson nodded, "They have a lot of concerts there."

Aunt Mariah looked confused, "At a hockey rink?"

Both Patterson and Nora nodded.

"Your Uncle Theo and I loved live music,"
Mariah reminisced. "I don't care how good of
a sound system you have, recorded music never
sounds as good as live music when being there
in person."

The two younger people agreed.

"Have you ever been to the Chicago
Symphony?" Mariah asked Nora.

Nora shook her head no.

"Oh, we used to go there as often as we could.
It's wonderful," Mariah sat smiling for a
second. "We must all go together sometime.
It's best around Christmas. You haven't heard
Christmas music until you've heard it played by
a really good symphony orchestra."

"I would love that," Nora sighed.

"Then we'll have to do that," insisted Aunt
Mariah.

The three chatted about Christmas in general
for the next few minutes and then Aunt Mariah
asked Nora what she did for a living. This was
just the opening that Nora and Patterson were
waiting for.

"Nora is a secretary at an insurance company," replied Patterson.

"That sounds boring," consoled Aunt Mariah.

"Not at all," corrected Nora. "I work in the fraud investigation division. I type up all the reports from the investigators. You'd be surprised how interesting it is."

"I bet it is," replied Aunt Mariah.

"In the year that I've been working there I've transcribed reports of jewelry and art thefts, fake deaths, and even murders," Nora proclaimed.

Aunt Mariah was astounded, "Murders? You would think that would be taken care of by the police."

"Sometimes it's made to look like an accident or natural causes. It's almost always a close friend or family member, someone that the victim knows and trusts. Private physicians never expect or even consider foul play," Nora went on. "There was this one case, about six months ago, where this guy in his late fifties married a woman ten years younger than him. The guy was loaded and had never been married before. A little more than a year after he got married, he died of a massive heart

attack. The family doctor signed the death
certificate and everything. The guy was even
buried when the insurance claim was made.
The investigator did a standard background
check on the wife and found that she had been
married twice before. Her first husband had
gotten dizzy while going down into the
basement, tripped on a broken step, and broke
his neck. Her second husband had experienced
a massive heart attack, very much like her third
husband. The investigator brought it to the
police, and it was enough to get the body
exhumed. Sure enough, when the forensic
pathologist did an autopsy, he found traces of
some sort of drug that causes a heart attack.
The police found that the wife had a cousin that
was a druggist. It turns out that they were in on
the whole thing from the very start.”

“What a horrible thing to happen,” Aunt Mariah
gasped. “But it’s so easy for an attractive
woman to take advantage of a man.”

“It happens to women also,” returned Nora.
“There was this lady who’s husband was a
jeweler. The poor man was killed in a holdup
at his shop. The woman was young and soon
remarried. About a year after her marriage
there was a break in at their home. Her new
husband was away on business. It was at night,
and she was all alone. Her husband kept a

revolver in a drawer near the bed. When she heard the noise downstairs, she took out the gun, went down the stairs, and confronted the burglar. She took a shot at the guy. Of course, she missed. The guy returned fire, killing her.”

“Oh, my God!” exclaimed Aunt Mariah.

“Neighbors heard the shots and called the police,” Nora resumed. “Well, during any homicide investigation they run ballistics on all the bullets that they find. It turns out that one of the bullets matched the one that had killed the woman’s first husband.”

“You mean that the burglar was the same man that had robbed her first husband’s shop?” asked the mortified Aunt.

Nora shook her head, “No, the matching bullet was the one that they dug out of the wall, the one from the second husband’s revolver.”

A look of horror came over Aunt Mariah’s face, “She had married the man that killed her husband!”

Nora smiled and nodded, “Aint that a kick in the head. The investigation revealed that the two men had planned the entire thing.”

Mariah sat quietly with a strange look of concern on her face.

"I think that we should talk about something a little less gruesome," sighed Patterson.

"Indeed," agreed Aunt Mariah.

"Nora and I have been doing a lot of sailing this summer," Patterson said, to change the subject.

"It's been so long since I've been sailing," lamented Aunt Mariah dreamily.

"You should come with us some day," suggested Nora.

"Yes, why not?" agreed Patterson.

Aunt Mariah sat contemplating for several seconds, "That would be very nice. You know your father would take me sailing every weekend during the summer when we were in high school and college."

"I know," said Patterson.

"He was such a good big brother to me," Aunt Mariah sighed nostalgically.

"And he still would be if you let him," impressed Patterson.

Aunt Mariah heard, but ignored the comment, "We had such wonderful Christmases."

"I remember when I was little," Patterson joined. "It was nice."

Aunt Mariah sat quietly as if in a trance.

"I understand that you are having hypnotherapy to help you sleep," Nora finally said.

Aunt Mariah snapped back into the conversation, "Oh, yes."

"Is it helping?" wondered Patterson.

Aunt Mariah nodded, "Yes, I slept wonderfully Friday night, and not badly last night. I have another treatment on Monday."

"Wow, I don't think that I could ever let anyone hypnotize me," laughed Nora.

"I used to feel exactly the same way," agreed Aunt Mariah. "But Professor Corrothers reassured me that you cannot make anyone do anything that they don't really want to do through hypnoses."

Nora laughed again, "That's the problem! There's so many things that I really want to do, but wont because they'd get me in trouble. I mean, like there are times that I'd really like to tell my boss to take a flying leap and shove it. Of course, that would get me fired."

Aunt Mariah and Patterson couldn't help but laugh.

Nora looked frustrated, "That could be a real problem."

"I should say so," chuckled Aunt Mariah.

"Did you say Professor Corrothers?" Patterson asked his aunt.

"Yes. Why?" returned Aunt Mariah.

"Nothing," said Patterson offhandedly. "It's just that I pass a church nearly everyday that has on its sign that the pastor is Reverend Carlton A. Corrothers."

"Yancy introduced him as Professor. I don't think that I got his first name," Aunt Mariah returned.

"I suppose there are a lot of people named Corrothers, I wonder if these two are related?" considered Patterson casually.

"Dinner is served," announced Stanton.

The conversation ended as the three went in for
dinner.

Chapter Eleven

More than the Weather Heats Up

It was a long and delightful dinner with a wide variety of light dinner talk going on between the three. By the time that cake and coffee were served in the living room, it was late, and Patterson and Nora announced that it was time for them to leave. Aunt Mariah thanked them for having come. She politely escorted them to the door and said that it was very nice to have them and that they should do it again soon. Nora and Patterson thanked her and agreed that they would do it again soon. The two then went to Patterson's car.

It was a few moments before the two began to talk as Patterson drove.

"I think that went very well," said Nora. "Not only do I think that we accomplished what we had intended to do, it was a nice evening also."

Patterson agreed, "It did go extremely well on all levels. Those two stories that you told were excellent. Did you see the expression on her face?"

"I think that we planted the seeds of doubt alright," Nora concurred.

"I didn't know that you had such a great imagination," Patterson complimented.

"I didn't make those stories up. They're from actual cases that the Clarks have worked," Nora revealed.

"My God!" exclaimed Patterson. "That is scary!"

"Do you really pass a church with a sign that says that the pastor is Reverend Carlton A. Corrothers?" wondered Nora.

"No, I just remembered that Jackie had said that one of Gates' known associates was a Reverend Carlton A. Corrothers and thought that I'd throw that in for good measure," Patterson answered. "I really got a kick when you said that you were afraid to get hypnotized because you might do something like tell your boss to take a flying leap."

"Oh, that part was real," Nora snickered. "I was going to say sleep with my boyfriend, but I figured that that would have been in poor taste."

"That boat has long sailed anyway," added Patterson.

Nora gave him an angry gaze.

Monday, August 25, was the first day of the last week of the month. The mercury would climb to 82 degrees by midafternoon, although it was ten degrees cooler when Phyllis and Benjamin arrived at the office. As usual, Phillip was already there and complaining about the coffee. He grabbed three donuts and called the Attlees into his office, adding that they should grab their own donuts it they wanted any. They didn't.

"I want the two of you to look into a case that I've assigned Jackie and Duck to," Phillip said as they all sat down.

Phyllis was surprised that her grandfather had given the two apprentices a case to work on their own. Phillip went on to explain the particulars of the case, adding that it seemed like a nice easy fraud case with no real danger involved, and that's why he figured that it would be a good case for the two rookies to cut their teeth on. Phyllis agreed.

"I just want the two of you to keep an eye on them to make sure that this don't blow up into something bigger. Some cases have a way of doing that," Phillip requested.

Phyllis and Benjamin agreed that they could keep tabs on the two youngsters.

"Be discreet, I don't want them to think that I don't trust them, but I don't trust them," Phillip chuckled.

Phyllis and Benjamin chuckled and agreed.

"Too bad that the two of you didn't go to yesterday's game at Wrigley. The Cubs won one to nothing," Phillip said changing the subject.

It was two hours later when Yancy Gates arrived at the Emmerson house. As usual, Stanton let him in. Mariah was reading in the library.

"Good morning, Mariah," greeted Gates cheerfully. "How'd your dinner go last night?"

"It was quite nice," Mariah answered. "Patterson's young lady is very nice."

"My ears were itching last night did you talk about me?" Gates asked.

Mariah shook her head, "Oh, Yancy, don't be so conceited. We talked about everything but you."

"Really, Patterson seemed so interested in my abilities when we met," Gates reminded.

"He's much more interested in his young lady friend's abilities than anything else, if you ask me," Mariah chuckled.

"Alas, young love," Gates snickered. "So, what does Patterson's young lady do for a living?"

Mariah thought for a second, "I believe that she said that she was a secretary at some insurance company."

"How boring, poor girl," yawned Gates. "What else did I miss?"

"We talked about Christmases when Patterson was small and how I used to go sailing with his father all the time before I was married. They invited me to go sailing with them," replied Mariah.

"Sailing!" exclaimed Gates. "That's a splendid idea. Ocean air is just what you need."

"I hate to say this, but it's a lake not an ocean," Mariah reminded.

Gates laughed, "I know, but we should take an ocean voyage. It would do you wonders. We could go to the Bahamas or Hawaii. Better yet, we fly to Venice and then sail the Mediterranean for a month or so."

"That sounds like a very nice plan," Mariah sighed dreamily. "We should do that right after the Christmas holidays."

Gates looked disgruntled, "Nonsense! We should do it now."

"But it would be so much more appreciated when it's freezing here in Chicago," chuckled Mariah.

"You need to do this now," insisted Gates. "You need to get out of this museum full of memories."

Mariah looked sad, "But they are such nice memories."

"You need to stop living in the past," Gates persisted. "Theo wants you to go on with your life. He wants you to make new memories."

"That's what Theo wants?" sighed Mariah.

"Yes, he's gone and never coming back. It's time to make a new life for yourself," Gates scolded.

"I suppose that there is something to what you say," moaned Mariah as she looked out the window of the library. "How soon could you leave?"

"Tomorrow, if need be," returned Gates.

Mariah looked shocked, "Good Lord! I never asked, it was none of my business, but what do you do for a living that you could get away tomorrow?"

Gates looked befuddled for an instant, "I'm…a… I'm an investor. I live off of the interest and dividends that I make off my investments."

The corners of Mariah's mouth turned up slightly, "It must be very handy to be clairvoyant for an investor. Hardly seems very fair, but then, what is fair in the world of business?"

"It doesn't work like that," Gates contended.

"Well, if you ever divine a good stock tip, don't hesitate to clue me into it," laughed Mariah.

Gates looked as if he was temporarily lost in thought, "Indeed I will. In fact, I'd be happy to help you out with your portfolio."

Mariah smiled, "Peterson, Whitcomb, and Rice have taken care of our investments for two generations, I see no reason to switch now."

"Of course," smiled Gates. "But I am psychic, and I wouldn't ever think of charging you any fees or commissions."

"Theo always felt that it was best to keep friendships and business separate," Mariah ventured.

"Yes, I know," Gates said slowly. "He's most likely right."

Gates looked at his watch, "Oh my goodness, I didn't realize that it was so late. I offered to pick up Carlton and drive him up here for your session today."

"Carlton?" queried Mariah.

"Yes, Professor Corrothers," Gates informed her. "His first name is Carlton. Why?"

Mariah shook her head, "No reason, I just didn't recall you mentioning the Professor's first name."

"Sorry, I guess that I didn't," apologized Gates. "I really have to run now."

Yancy Gates quickly left the Emmerson house. After he was gone, Mariah rang for Stanton.

"You rang?" Stanton asked as he entered.

Mariah looked concerned, "I hate to take advantage of your years of loyal service, but under the circumstances I don't feel that I have a choice."

Stanton looked at his boss caringly, "I have always felt that I am more than just a servant here, Madam. You have always treated me as if I were a good friend or part of your family. I would do anything for you or your late husband."

"I'm beginning to have my concerns about Mr. Gates' true intentions," Mariah Emmerson professed. "There are some things that my nephew's young lady said last night that opened my eyes."

"Indeed, Madam," agreed Stanton. "What shall be required of me, Mrs. Emmerson?"

"Good Lord, John," Mariah sighed. "My name is Mariah, you are a member of this family, please, call me Mariah."

"Yes, Mada…Mariah," choked Stanton.

"When Yancy and that Professor fellow return, keep an eye on me," Mariah advocated. "Whatever happens, don't let me leave the house with them. If I ask you to give me any money, or I ask for my checkbook, say, 'there is no money in the house', or, 'the checkbook was lost, and the new ones have not yet arrived'. If they force me to go with them, call my nephew or my brother."

"How about the police?" asked Stanton.

Mariah thought for a second and nodded.

Stanton left Mariah's company and went directly to the servant's quarters and called Patterson. When there was no answer, he called the number that Patterson had given him for Nora, at the Clark offices. She was there. Stanton advised Nora of what Mariah had just asked him to do. Nora thanked him and relayed the message to Duck, who immediately left for the Emmerson home. Unknown to Duck, Phyllis was right behind him.

Chapter Twelve

A Change of Plans

Yancy Gates had to hurry to get to Professor Corrothers' 'church' before Corrothers would have to leave for his appointment at the Emmerson mansion. Corrothers was surprised to see him.

"I think that we might have to expedite our timetable somewhat," Gates advised his compatriot.

Corrothers looked at him quizzically, "What's up?"

"I'm afraid that the stupid nosy kid has been planting seeds of distrust in his idiot Aunt's very limited brain," Gates related.

"I was afraid of that when you told me about the fact that he had studied parapsychology," Corrothers lamented. "You should have been there last night to put him off track."

"I believed that it was a no win situation," replied Gates.

"Well, this certainly isn't much better," complained Corrothers.

"Don't worry about the kid," Gates reassured. "I'll take care of that little creep."

"So, what do you want from me?" inquired Corrothers.

"You're going to have to step up the hypnotherapy," pressed Gates.

"I can't do that!" protested Corrothers. "I can't just say, 'You are asleep. I want you to give all your money to Yancy.' Or, 'I want you to marry Yancy.' Or, how about, 'I want you to donate all your money to the Church of Blessed Deliverance.' You know that it doesn't work like that."

"I need her to either let me take over her investments or to go on a cruise with me," Gates demanded. "I either have to get her away from her family or get as much money as I can, as quickly as I can, before this all falls apart on us."

Corrothers shook his head, "It's not that easy. It takes time."

"You've done it before!" argued Gates.

"Yes, with the use of drugs," agreed Corrothers. "And that is so risky. I almost got caught last time."

"You better think of a way, or you are going to make me very angry, and you know what happens when I get angry," scowled Gates.

"You remember we're facing a murder charge if we get caught," warned Corrothers.

"You're facing a murder charge. You're the one who gave him the drugs. Remember?" Gates growled.

"I should have never gotten involved with you," lamented Corrothers.

"You never minded when you got your cut of the score," reminded Gates.

Corrothers scowled as Gates hustled him to the car. The two then left together for the Emmerson home.

Duck recognized Gates' car as it turned north onto Sheridan Road in front of him. Duck figured that there was no reason to be careful, as Gates had no reason to suspect that he was under any sort of surveillance. The only evasive action that Duck took was to drive past the Emmerson driveway and head around to the tradesmen's entrance. Phyllis was stuck trying to find a parking place on the narrow winding road. She pulled off into a stand of trees, about an eighth of a mile past where Duck had turned, and walked back to the house.

Stanton opened the door for Gates and Corrothers and then went to see who was making a delivery at the tradesman's entrance. Stanton was relieved when the shaggy looking hippy at the door showed the butler his state investigator's apprentice license. Stanton quickly apprised Duck of what was going on. Duck asked if there was a place where he could be able to hide safely that was close enough so he could also hear what was being said. Stanton led Duck down into the huge basement and over to a vent grate in the low ceiling. With the help of a step stool, Duck was able to get his ear right up to the grate. He could hear everything as plainly as if he were in the room. He then instructed Stanton to go back upstairs and attend to whatever might be needed by the visitors.

From Duck's hiding place, he could plainly hear Professor Corrothers place Mariah into the hypnotic trance. He could hear Corrothers telling her that she would sleep soundly and peacefully. He then heard Corrothers begin telling her how her late husband Theo was happy that she and Yancy were getting along so well together. Duck heard Corrothers tell her that Theo wanted her to be happy and that all

Yancy wanted for her was happiness and well-being. Corrothers continued to tell Mariah that Theo wanted her to trust Yancy. Then Corrothers began to talk about waves, soothing waves. He talked about drifting easily and carelessly on rolling waves, rocking gently to sleep on soft, slow, swells of ocean waves. He continued this line for some time. Duck was starting to get sleepy himself. He almost fell off the stepstool. Then Duck heard Gates say something to Corrothers. The two seemed to be whispering, which made it difficult for Duck to hear. Suddenly he heard Corrothers speak more loudly, as if angry.

"That's all I can do now," Corrothers complained. "I don't carry those kind of drugs with me. You'll just have to set up another session."

Gates said something in return that Duck couldn't make out. It soon became obvious that the 'therapy' session was over, so Duck made his way back up to the servants' part of the house. He filled Stanton in on what he had heard and sat around to see what else, if anything, would happen. Nothing else happened. Gates soon left to take the Professor home. Duck decided that it was time that he should meet Mrs. Emmerson. Stanton guided him through the enormous house to where

Mariah Emmerson sat nervously in her favorite room, the solarium.

"Mariah," Stanton said as he entered the room, "I have a friend of Mr. Patterson's here for you to meet."

Mariah turned to see the disheveled looking Duck standing in the doorway.

"Mrs. Emmerson," Duck began. "You don't know me. My name is Duckworth Shetz, I am a friend of your nephew, Patterson, and his girlfriend. Nora and I work together."

"You work at an insurance company?" Mariah said skeptically.

Duck looked dismayed, "No, I'm afraid that we haven't been totally honest with you."

Mariah looked concerned.

"Yes, Patterson is dating Nora, but neither she nor I work at an insurance company. We both work for the Clark Detective Agency," Duck confessed. "Patterson was concerned about Yancy Gates, and he asked us to check him out."

"What do you do for the Clark Agency?" wondered Mariah.

"I know that I don't look like it, but I'm an investigator," Duck confided.

Mariah smiled, "I must say you don't look anything like Sam Spade or Micky Spillane. Although, I suppose that in their day, they appeared to look on the seedy side."

"I work undercover a lot," Duck chuckled. "Now, my boss does look like Sam Spade. You should meet him!"

"I look forward to it," Mariah grinned.

Duck continued, "At any rate, I'm sorry to say that we've discovered that Mr. Gates and Professor, or Reverend, Corrothers are both known con-artists."

"Why didn't Patterson tell me this?" asked Mariah.

Duck exhaled heavily, "We were concerned that if we had just confronted you with it, you would have rejected and resented our intrusion into your private life."

Mariah considered what Duck had said for several minutes.

"Were those stories that Nora related to me just made up?" questioned Mariah.

Duck shook his head, "No ma'am, everything that we related to you is absolute truth. As sad as they are, those stories were true."

"And what brought you here today?" wondered Mariah.

"Your nephew gave Stanton our number to call if he felt that there was anything to be concerned over," explained Duck.

"When you told me to make sure that you didn't leave the house with those men, or give them any money, I took it upon myself to call the detectives," confessed Stanton.

Mariah breathed heavily for a few moments, "You did very well, John. Thank you. And thank you also, Mr. Shetz. I must also thank my nephew."

"He loves you very much, Mrs. Emmerson," Duck returned.

"Did Patterson have to pay for your services?" Mariah asked.

Duck smiled, "Our boss said that if he didn't, the investigation would be illegal, so he charged him a dollar."

Mariah chuckled, "It would seem that I owe a lot of people a thank you."

"It's alright," laughed Duck.

"Is it all over now? I mean what comes next?" wondered Mariah.

"As these two con men did you no physical or financial harm, the police will have no cause to press any charges," Duck informed her.

"You mean that they would have had to hurt me in some way for the police to take any interest?" sighed Mariah indignantly.

"I'm afraid so," Duck confirmed. "That's the way it works. It's really not their fault, they're so busy that they couldn't go after every con-artist that tries to pull a con."

"I feel so invaded, so compromised," Mariah grumbled. "I wish that there was something that we could do to make them pay."

Duck rubbed his chin and shrugged his shoulders, "I guess that we could play along with them and see where it goes."

"I take it that you mean either go away with Yancy or give him money to invest and have him steal it," considered Mariah.

"I would seriously reject the idea of you going away with him," Duck offered. "He just wants to get you away from your family's influence so that he can convince you to marry him."

"And then I suppose that he'll slowly steal my money and then finally divorce me," pondered Mariah.

"More likely he'd have you meet with some sort of accident and die," returned Duck. "It's actually faster and easier."

"That's not very reassuring," whimpered Mariah.

"I don't suggest that course," recommended Duck.

"Then let's go for letting him steal my money," decided Mariah.

"There's no guarantee that we will be able to recover it all," offered Duck.

"That's alright, I have a very lot of money. I don't mind losing some of it to catch this scoundrel," Mariah returned.

"Ok," sighed Duck. "But this is way out of my experience. We need to have you talk to Mr. Clark and his granddaughter, Phyllis."

"What do I do when Yancy comes back today?" asked Mariah.

"We get you out of here," answered Duck. "I'll take you to our office and we can stash you somewhere safe. Stanton can tell him that you've gone to visit Patterson for a day or so."

"You don't think that Stanton will be in any danger?" wondered Mariah.

"Gates would be a fool to do anything that would expose him as a criminal," posed Duck.

"Don't be concerned for my well-being," Stanton interjected. "I served with the Royal Marines when I was young. I have a gun and I know how to use it. Believe me, I would love to have a reason to shoot Mr. Gates."

Phyllis had been watching the front door of the Emmerson house during all this. She had found a spot in the garden where she was in good cover and had an unobstructed view of both the front door and the tradesman's door. She was surprised when she observed Duck emerge with Mrs. Emmerson and drive her away in his car. She followed them all the way back to her office.

Chapter Thirteen

A Change of Heart

As Phyllis followed Duck and Mrs. Emmerson into the Uptown National Bank building, she wondered what in the world Duck was doing. By the time that she stepped into the office, Mrs. Emmerson and Duck were already in Phillip's private office.

"What's going on?" Phyllis asked Alice.

"Don't ask me! No one ever tells me anything," returned Alice.

Phillip's door opened and he called his granddaughter in.

"This is Mrs. Mariah Emmerson, Patterson's aunt," Phillip introduced. "She would like to engage our agency to help her catch a weasel."

Phyllis smiled and said hello.

"First, I'd like to know where my nephew is. I'm concerned for his safety," ventured Mariah.

"Don't worry, Mrs. Emmerson, we have one of our operatives following him," answered Phyllis.

At this point Duck elaborated on the circumstances which prompted him to bring Mariah into their offices. After the long explanation, Phillip leaned back in his highbacked, swivel chair and thought quietly for several moments.

Phillip said slowly, "So, as I gather, you are willing to go on posing as if you're being duped by Richard Gordon so that we can build a fraud case."

Mariah looked confused, "Who's Richard Gordon?"

Phillip smiled, "You know him as Yancy Gates."

"Yancy's not even his real name!" sighed Mariah.

Phillip shook his head, "I know that it hurts that you were taken in, but you were in a vulnerable state after the death of your husband. It's easy for unscrupulous crumbs like Gordon, uh, I mean, Yancy, to take advantage of widows."

Mariah's eyes filled with tears, "It's not just that I'm hurt, but I feel like such a fool. My brother and his family tried to help me, but I shut them out…for a handsome con-man! I'm such an old fool!"

Phillip and Phyllis looked at the pathetic weeping woman sympathetically. Duck placed his hand on her shoulder.

"You're not a fool, Mrs. Emmerson. You are a victim," Duck consoled softly.

Mariah sniffled loudly, "I refuse to be his victim. I want to do whatever I can to get that louse."

"You could be putting yourself in danger," informed Phyllis.

"At the very least, you could lose a lot of money," added Phillip.

Mariah swallowed hard, "I don't care. I want to get that bastard."

Meanwhile, Jackie had followed Patterson to the Church of Blessed Deliverance. Patterson was snooping around, not knowing exactly what he was looking for. He had not seen Gates come to get Corrothers. Nor had he seen them leave and then return. However, a 'devoted church worker' of Reverend Corrothers had definitely seen Patterson.

As Gates and Corrothers returned from the Emmerson house, Yancy drove the car into an underground parking lot. The two made their way up into the administrative part of the church building where they were met by Brother Dominic Thornton.

"There's some kid hanging around here, snooping," advised the henchman, Thornton. "He's been at it most of the day."

Gates immediately suspected that it was Patterson. He described Patterson to Thornton, who then verified that it was Patterson.

"That stupid kid is going to blow this entire operation," grumbled Gates.

Corrothers shook his head, "No, he's not."

Corrothers turned to Thornton, "Invite the young man in, make him feel comfortable, and then eliminate him."

"You want that he should sleep with the fishes?" verified Thornton.

"I want that he should disappear without any trace," confirmed Corrothers.

"Got it, Boss," affirmed Thornton.

Dominick Thornton quickly left to do his master's bidding. He carefully searched around the church grounds. He finally went out into a courtyard that was nestled between the three buildings that made up the church complex. There was a brick and stone wall that enclosed that courtyard on the east side. Patterson had climbed this wall and was now inside the courtyard. Thornton walked slowly among the many five and six foot high bushes with a few religious statues that filled the courtyard. The courtyard was a beautiful and quiet place. People who rented this church for weddings often had the pictures of the wedding party taken in this charming, picturesque sanctuary. There were dozens of places for Patterson to hide as he heard Thornton walk out into the haven. Thornton thought that he had heard something also as Patterson scrambled into the bushes to conceal himself. Patterson thought that he had found the perfect spot to go unnoticed by the gun wielding thug, however, Thornton had the advantage. It wasn't long before Patterson felt the barrel of a forty-five automatic pressing against his back. He nearly passed out with fear.

"Ok, step out of that shrub or I'll blast you right here," Thornton commanded. "It's not my first choice. I'd have a lot of cleaning to do, but I'll blow you to kingdom come right here and now if you make me."

Patterson swallowed hard, "Why should I make it easy on you? You're just going to kill me anyway. Might as well get it over with quickly."

"Whatever you say, kid," replied Thornton.

Patterson heard the blast of a gun going off, but he felt nothing. There was no pain. There was no feeling of his body being torn apart. He had heard that people felt cold when they had been shot and were dying, but he didn't feel cold. In fact, he was still standing. He hadn't even been moved by the force of the bullet. Suddenly, he realized that he had also heard a woman's voice yell, "Drop it, or I'll shoot!". And then there were two gun shots. There, on the ground at his feet, lay his assailant, dead. Patterson looked around. Off to the right stood Jackie, holding her Colt .38 special in her hand. She had followed Patterson over the wall, seen what was about to happen, and after her warning shout, had fired from the left side of where the assailant was standing when Thornton did not drop his weapon. Thornton was hit and thrown out of line of Patterson as he fired the gun.

"You killed him!" exclaimed Patterson.

"I couldn't take the chance that he'd kill you. I had to fire," explained Jackie. "Now let's get the hell out of here! Someone must have heard the gunshots.”

The two quickly jumped the wall and ran to their cars.

“Meet me at the Clark offices,” Jackie shouted as they drove off.

Patterson did as he was told and headed toward the Uptown neighborhood. However, Jackie, seeing that she was not being followed, stopped at the first pay phone that she spotted. Jackie quickly call the Clark offices.

“I’ve just killed a man at the Church of Blessed Deliverance,” Jackie told Alice.

Alice quickly transferred the call to Phillip’s phone. Phillip’s face grew livid with concern.

“Call Sean,” Phillip commanded Phyllis. “Tell him to get squads to that phony church on the double, Jackie just iced a guy there.”

Phyllis bolted into her office to call Captain O’Malley as Phillip got the details of what had happened.

Phillip told those standing there, “Don’t worry, both Jackie and Patterson are ok. Now, Duck, get Mrs. Emmerson on ice. Ben, grab your gat and come with me. Alice, when that kid, Patterson, gets here, have him stay put. Even if you gotta tie him up, keep him here! And make sure that your piece is loaded."

Alice nodded as everyone scrambled to do as they were told. Phyllis, Benjamin, and Phillip rushed to their cars and went to meet Jackie and Sean at the Church of Blessed Deliverance.

At the Church of Blessed Deliverance complex, Reverend Corrothers dashed into Gates' office.

"Grab everything important," Corrothers shouted. "We got to get out of here."

Gates looked at his partner with alarm.

"Thornton is dead!" Corrothers yelled.

"Don't get so panicked," sighed Gates calmly. "Just have the staff clean it up."

"You don't understand! After the gunshots, some of the staff saw that kid and some dame jump the wall and head for their cars," Corrothers insisted feverously.

"They got away?" Gates bellowed in alarm.

"We're in deep trouble this time," impressed Corrothers.

Gates grabbed some papers, a wad of cash, and a gun, and scurried to join Corrothers running to the garage. The sound of police cars grew louder and louder. The two jumped into Yates' car and headed up the exit ramp. A police cruiser blocked their escape. In a flash, several officers with drawn weapons surrounded the culprits' car. Other officers stopped anyone from exiting the church grounds.

Within minutes, Captain O'Malley and the Flynn brothers arrived at the scene. They made their way to the courtyard to find the lifeless body of Dominick Thornton in a pool of blood.

"Looks like Phyllis was here," commented Jack Flynn.

O'Malley sneered, "Actually, it was Jackie."

"That cute little girl did this?" chuckled Steve Flynn.

"Phyllis trained her well," added Jack.

"Ok, I want every inch of this place searched," commanded O'Malley. "Anything that is at all out of the ordinary for a church building is tagged as evidence."

An army of police officers flooded the complex. The employees were all escorted into waiting police wagons and taken to be interviewed and possibly booked. The legion of police began to scour the facilities.

Phillip, Phyllis, and Benjamin arrived at the crime scene. After a few minutes thcy were escorted to where O'Malley was directing the activity.

"What in God's name is going on here?" O'Malley challenged as he saw the three.

Phyllis began to explain to O'Malley as Steve Flynn approached them.

"We just discovered a large cache of weapons in the basement and under the alter, enough to start a small revolution!" the detective advised his boss.

"We got all sorts of pharmaceuticals in a storage room," added Jack Flynn.

"It seems that these guys were into everything," uttered Phillip softly.

"This is some operation," Phyllis agreed. "Which just makes me wonder…"

Both Phillip and Sean gazed at her expectantly.

"It seems to me that con men with this amount of skill wouldn't be waiting around reading the obituaries looking for a really good mark, such as Mariah Emmerson. These are the sort of guys that make their own opportunities," Phyllis considered.

"I think that you're onto something there sweetheart," agreed Phillip.

"What are the two of you talking about?" inquired Captain Sean O'Malley.

"It could be that these gonzos planned on taking the Emmerson fortune from the very start," Phillip posed. "They singled out Theodore and Mariah Emmerson as easy targets. Somehow they managed to cause Theodore's heart attack so that they could move in on Mariah."

"Mariah said that Yancy Gates knew things about her husband that were very private, such as the fact that he was addicted to nicotine and was desperately struggling to give up smoking. He also knew that Theodore had been attending meetings at a smokers' support group. And there were other things also," Phyllis advised.

"Ok, so this guy Gates somehow knew Theodore Emmerson. But, how do you cause the guy to have a heart attack?" questioned O'Malley.

"There are several drugs that will cause or imitate a heart attack," offered Phillip.

O'Malley shook his head, "But they all work instantly or nearly instantly. Emmerson was at home with his wife for hours before he went up to exercise and have his heart attack."

"Aconite," moaned Phyllis.

"Wolfsbane?" asked O'Malley.

"That can kill you instantly," advised Phillip.

"Aconite, given in trace amounts, given over a prolonged period of time, interacts with voltage-dependent sodium channels which are proteins present in the membranes of all cardiac and neural cells. Aconite causes the cardiac cells not to be able to repolarize, eventually leading to a heart attack," Phyllis replied.

Phillip and O'Malley looked at each other.

"I want everyone to be on the lookout for bottles labeled aconite, wolfsbane, Monk's blood, or Devil's helmet," shouted O'Malley.

"Also, look for anything labeled as appetite suppressants, or labeled as being for 'the suppression of nicotine craving'," added Phyllis.

Chapter Fourteen

The Plot Thickens

About the same time that Phillip, Phyllis, and Benjamin had arrived at the Church of Blessed Deliverance, Patterson was walking into the Clark offices.

"Where's my aunt?" was the first thing that Patterson said.

Alice relaxed her grip on the Colt forty-five automatic pistol which was hidden in her top right desk drawer.

"Duck's got her stashed in a safe house," Alice replied.

"I've got to see her," demanded Patterson.

"No, you don't 'gotta' see her!" returned Alice sternly. "What you 'gotta' do is cool your heels here until the Clarks get back."

"You don't understand," shouted Patterson franticly. "Someone just tried to kill me, and Jackie shot him to death."

"We know all about that, sonny," sighed Alice coolly. "That's where everyone's at right now."

Patterson stared at Alice with disbelief.

"What you need to do is sit down, cool down, calm down, and pull yourself together," Alice said sternly. "Have yourself a cup of coffee."

Patterson began to settle down, "No, thank you."

"I said drink some coffee!" demanded Alice.

Patterson poured himself a cup of coffee and sipped it.

"My God! This is lousy coffee," Patterson uttered.

Alice looked at him contemptuously, "Everybody's a food critic."

As Patterson made himself comfortable for his wait, Nora arrived at the office. Her Aunt Alice had called her and brought her up to speed on the day's events. Patterson was happy to see Nora as she hugged him and then sat next to him, holding his hand. The time passed slowly as Patterson and Nora waited for Phillip, Phyllis, and Benjamin to return. It was after seven in the evening when the four walked into the office. Patterson jumped to his feet.

"Where's Jackie? Is she alright?" Patterson babbled excitedly. "Is that guy really dead?"

Phillip looked at the trembling college student, "Yeah, the goon's really dead. Jackie's at the 18th, filling out reports with Captain O'Malley. She's fine, at least as fine as you can be right after killing some guy."

"This is all my fault," wailed Patterson. "I did it again. If I hadn't gone sticking my nose in where it didn't belong, none of this would have ever happened."

"That's alright, Kiddo," Phillip consoled. "It worked out for the best, this time."

Patterson was astonished.

"The shooting gave O'Malley 'just cause' to conduct a search of the grounds," Benjamin told Patterson. "During the search, they found a stash of illegal weapons, a huge horde of narcotics, and other restricted drugs. They found drugs that may turn out to be the cause of your uncle's heart attack."

"We need to do a search of your Aunt's house to see if your uncle was using any kind of

pharmaceuticals to help him quit smoking,"
interjected Phyllis.

"He was," muttered Patterson. "I remember, he
told me that some guy that he knew from the
support group that he was going to gave him a
whole bunch of pills to help."

"Do you think that some of them are still
around the house?" asked Phyllis.

Patterson scrunched his forehead, "I would
imagine so. My aunt hasn't let anyone touch
any of his things, even though Gates was telling
her that the sooner that she got rid of that stuff,
the quicker she would start to recover."

"He wanted her to get rid of the evidence,"
asserted Phillip.

"Evidence?" gulped Patterson.

"I'm sorry to tell you this, but we think that
those pills were laced with a drug that
eventually caused your uncle's heart attack,"
Benjamin told Patterson.

Patterson's eyes began to fill with tears, "God
no!"

"I know, Kiddo," consoled Phillip. "It's one
thing to believe that he died of a natural cause,

but it's a whole other ballgame to find out that he was murdered."

"How could that be?" lamented Patterson.

"We think that Gates and Corrothers planned this whole thing from the very beginning. Somehow, they found out that your uncle was seeing a cardiologist and had been advised to quit smoking and to begin to exercise. That made him vulnerable, and they moved in," Phyllis offered.

As Patterson processed everything that he'd just been told, Phillip had Alice call the safe house to get permission to search the Emmerson house. Mariah gave it without hesitation.

"It would probably make things easier if you came along," Phyllis told Patterson.

"By the time we get there, it's going to be very late, and Pat was nearly killed today. Wouldn't it be ok if you waited till morning?" Nora questioned with concern.

"The sooner we get the goods and turn them over to Sean, the better," replied Phillip.

"Can't Captain O'Malley just send some officers over to do the search?" wondered Nora.

"Winnetka is out of his jurisdiction," returned Benjamin. "And the local police would want to wait for a court order, which would take forever. Whereas, we have the permission of our client, the homeowner."

"It's alright, I'm so wound up that I couldn't sleep if my life depended on it," added Patterson.

"Call Sean and let him know what we're doing," Phillip instructed Alice. "And make sure that the papers that you have Mrs. Emmerson sign tomorrow are dated yesterday! We don't need to complicate anything."

Alice nodded and went into the outer office.

Nora looked at Patterson, "If you're ok with this, I'm coming along."

Patterson said that he was, and he and Nora went with Phyllis, Benjamin, and Phillip to conduct the search.

It was nearly ten-thirty in the evening when the four arrived back at the Emmerson house. Stanton was still awake and quickly let them in. He was holding a thirty-eight revolver in his right hand. Each of the detectives went to different rooms to search. Phillip went to the exercise room with Stanton, while Benjamin

went to the master bedroom with Patterson.
Phyllis and Nora went into the bathroom to
check out the medicine cabinet.

"Are we looking for those little pink pills that
the master was taking to stop his cravings for
those coffin nails?" Stanton asked Phillip.

"That's right," answered Phillip. "Did you ever
see him taking them?"

Stanton nodded, "Yes, sir, all the time. I once
told him that if the cigarettes didn't kill him
those drugs would."

"You were very right, Stanton. They did,"
Phillip confirmed.

Stanton looked bewildered.

"This was a very elaborate scheme to enable
Yancy Gates to get into Mrs. Emmerson's life
and swindle her out of everything," informed
Phillip.

"I got them," Benjamin shouted from the
master bedroom.

Everyone rushed into the hall outside the
master bedroom as Benjamin and Patterson
came out with two small pill bottles full of pills,

labeled exactly like the ones found at the Church of Blessed Deliverance.

"Are these the pills that you saw Mr. Emmerson taking for his smoking addiction?" Phillip asked Stanton.

Stanton said that they were.

"Are you willing to testify to that in court?" pursued Phillip.

"Why, yes, with pleasure," confirmed Stanton.

"Mission accomplished," sighed Phillip with relief. "I'll run these over to Sean's office."

Phillip headed south to the 18th precinct while Benjamin and Phyllis drove Patterson and Nora to their respective homes and then went home themselves.

When Phillip arrived at the 18th, it was Sergeant Steve Flynn who was waiting to receive the pills.

"Been a long day for you," commented Phillip.

Steve chuckled, "They're all long days, lately."

Phillip laughed.

"Sean says that he'll have Henderson do the lab work first thing in the morning," Steve told Phillip.

Phillip laughed, "Not too early, I hope. It's been a long day for me, too, and I ain't as young as I used to be."

"Tell me about it," snickered Steve.

The two said goodnight and Phillip went to the office to sleep, instead of going home.

Earlier, when Jackie had left the police station, she went over to the safe house where Duck was guarding Mariah Emmerson. Jackie was feeling bad about having to kill the goon at the Church of Blessed Deliverance. She really wanted to see her boyfriend, Duck. When she got there, Duck held her in his arms tightly and kissed her.

"It's such an awful feeling knowing that you ended someone's life," Jackie cried.

"I know, but you did what you had to do," comforted Duck. "If you hadn't, he would have certainly killed you. And I bet he wouldn't be crying over it."

Jackie nodded as she hugged Duck and continued crying.

Mariah Emmerson was sitting in the kitchen drinking coffee. She heard Jackie and Duck talking and eagerly waited to find out about everything that had happened that day. But she recognized that she should give the two some time to get their emotions in hand. It took over a half hour before Jackie and Duck went into the kitchen. It was Jackie who detailed the events of the very long day. At the end of Jackie's discourse, they all sat staring at each other for some time. It was Mariah who broke the silence.

"It was those worms that killed Theo, not the cigarettes," sighed Mariah.

Duck nodded, "Yep, but the cigarettes made it all possible."

"I guess that this means that I will not have to pretend to be Yancy's stooge any longer?" asked Mariah.

"No, even if they can't get him for the murder, they got plenty of other stuff on him and Corrothers. They got enough to put them away for a long time," Duck answered.

"I'd really like to see them burn," spit out Mariah hatefully.

"I know. So would I," offered Duck sympathetically. "Maybe we can get Jackie to shoot the two of them."

"Very funny," choked out Jackie. "But as bad as I feel right now, I think that I could muster up enough hate to do it if I ever had them in my sites."

Mariah smiled, "Thank you, dear, but I'll be content with whatever the law does to them. Their dying won't ever bring back Theo."

"But that's what they deserve," offered Jackie.

Duck and Mariah looked somber and nodded slowly.

Chapter Fifteen

Wrapping it All Up in a Nice Package with a Bow

Tuesday, August 26th, Benjamin and Phyllis arrived late at the office. As they walked in, they asked Alice if Phillip was in yet.

"Are you kidding? We slept here last night," related Alice groggily.

Phyllis told Alice to go home. Benjamin offered to drive her. Alice happily accepted.

"Before you leave, did we hear anything from the police yet?" Phyllis asked.

Alice shook her head, "No, and we also have not heard a peep from Nora, Duck, or Mrs. Emmerson. We really need to get that Emmerson dame's John Hancock on this contract before the district attorney starts nosing around, putting together his case. Remember, without this contract signed on Sunday, we conducted an illegal investigation. I really doubt that the dollar business that Phillip did with Doctor Strange is going to hold up when the D.A. starts looking into that search that you conducted last night, or Patterson's break in at the Church of Blessed Deliverance, or the subsequent shooting and killing of one of their official workers."

Phyllis nodded, "I know. Gramps really was outside the lines on this one."

"It ain't the first time, sweetie," yawned Alice. "Before you were born, we were always right on the edge."

Phyllis shook her head. Benjamin escorted Alice out to his car. Phyllis settled down into the chair at Alice's desk. It was nearly one in the afternoon when Duck, Jackie, and Mrs. Emmerson arrived at the office. Jackie took over at the front desk, while Phyllis had Mrs. Emmerson sign all the necessary papers. It was about that time when Phillip finally awoke and ventured into the outer office.

"Jackie!" Phillip said with surprise. "How are you doing, Sweetheart?"

"Pretty good now, Mr. Clark," replied Jackie.

"You did good, don't feel bad about it," Phillip offered.

"I know. It just feels funny," Jackie sighed.

"I know, it always does," Phillip conceded.

"I made some fresh coffee," advised Jackie.

"You're a good detective and I'm happy to have you in the field, but I really miss your coffee," Phillip chuckled.

Jackie smiled, as the phone rang. Jackie answered it. After exchanging a few words, she thanked Lieutenant Jack Flynn and hung up the phone.

"Well?" asked Phillip as he poured some coffee.

"That was Lieutenant Flynn," Jackie announced. "He said he just got the lab report from Henderson. The pills that you recovered from the Emmerson house were laced with a very tiny amount of aconite and perfectly matched those seized in Captain O'Malley's raid of the Church of Blessed Deliverance. The dosage of the pills, the trace amount of aconite in each tablet, even the labeling on the containers, all matched. He says that the D.A. says that all we have to do is make a link between Emmerson and the two suspects and he can get a conviction."

"That's great," sighed Phillip.

"According to Mariah, Theodore went to his support group Tuesday and Thursday evenings at North Shore Community Center," inserted Phyllis, who'd come out of her office when she heard the phone ring. "I should go over there this evening and talk to the group leader."

"That's right," agreed Phillip. "Patterson said that his uncle told him that he had gotten the pills from a guy in his support group," remembered Phillip.

The North Shore Community Smokers' Support Group met at 8:00 p.m. Phyllis and Benjamin arrived at the meeting a few minutes early so that they could speak with the leader. The therapist who led the group was a tall, middle aged man, with horn rimmed glasses, and gray streaked hair. His name was Peter Manfred. At first, Peter was reluctant to speak to the private detectives, but reconsidered when Phyllis assured him that if he didn't talk to her that evening, he would have to talk to a police detective the next day. Peter Manfred looked at the picture of Theodore Emmerson and recognized him instantly.

"That's Mr. Emmerson," Peter offered. "I understand that he passed away a couple of weeks ago. I was so sorry to hear about it. He was a nice man. He was having such a tough time struggling with his nicotine addiction. You know it's so hard, especially for someone his age. Like most smokers from his generation, he'd been smoking since he was in eighth grade. To make it even worse, in his day it was socially acceptable, unlike pot, heroin and cocaine. And until relatively recently, no one thought that it was even harmful."

Phyllis then showed him pictures of Yancy Gates and Carlton Corrothers.

"Yes, of course, I know both of these men," Peter admitted.

This one is Nick…something…Nick Albert. He was a member of the same group that Mr. Emmerson came to. As a matter of fact, I think that they were friends. They would often go out together after the meetings," Peter offered. "Funny, Nick stopped coming right around the time that Mr. Emmerson died."

"And the other man?" asked Phyllis. "Oh, that's Reverend Carlton Corrothers. He sometimes gives motivational lectures to my groups."

"Did you ever notice that he also went out with Emmerson and Nick Albert?" Phyllis asked.

Peter Manfred scrunched his forehead as he thought for a few moments, "Yes, I believe so. Yes, he did on several occasions. I think that

Nick was a member of his church and that's why he took such an interest in Theodore."

"If you were called upon to testify to what you've just told me, would you do that?" asked Phyllis.

Peter Manfred looked confused for a second, "Yes, I suppose so. Why?"

Phyllis breathed hard, "I hate to tell you this, but we have reason to believe that these two men are responsible for the death of Theodore Emmerson."

A look of shock and horror swept over Peter Manfred's face, "My God, no!"

"In fact, the two are in custody as we speak," advised Phyllis. "You can expect a Sergeant Steve Flynn to be calling on you after your meeting this evening."

"Am I in any sort of trouble?" gasped Manfred. "Do I need a lawyer?"

Phyllis shook her head, "No, Sir. You've done nothing wrong. He'll just need to have you make a statement as to the facts that you've already told me."

Manfred nodded, "That's a relief."

"Do you encourage any of your group members to use any kind of drugs to help them kick the habit?" asked Benjamin.

Manfred looked aghast, "No never! That's just trading one addiction for another. I would never condone that. I'm a responsible therapist."

"Then you were not aware that either the man that you know as Nick Albert, or Reverend Corrothers, were doing just that?" addressed Benjamin.

Manfred looked dismayed, "No! I had no idea."

"Then you have no problems with the police," reassured Benjamin.

"Had I known that they were doing that, I'd have barred them from the group," insisted Manfred. "I'll be happy to cooperate with the police."

Phyllis and Benjamin thanked Peter Manfred and left. As they had conveyed to Mr. Manfred, at the end of his meeting that night, Sergeant Steve Flynn appeared to take his statement.

Wednesday morning Captain O'Malley invited Phyllis, Benjamin, and Phillip to join him for lunch at Mrs. Rice's Hotdog emporium.

"It's been a while since we all did this together," reminisced O'Malley. "Did you know, Ben, that…"

"You used to take Phyllis here after Cubs' games when she was little," Benjamin finished.

"I guess that you've heard about that," sighed O'Malley.

Benjamin chuckled.

As the four sat down to their hotdogs and Green River soda, O'Malley expressed that he'd had a long discussion with the district attorney that morning.

O'Malley reported, "The D.A. says that the only places that a forensic lab can recover signs of Aconite poisoning is in body fluids, and since those are removed during the embalming process, it's way too late for that. However, since the family physician recorded cause of death as ventricular tachycardia resulting in cardiac arrest, we shouldn't have much of a problem, as that is the usual cause of death from Aconite poisoning. Good news is that we will not have to exhume the body. Since we have chemically exact samples, both from the possession of drugs from Corrothers and Richard Gordon, aka Yancy Gates, and the possession of the drugs used by Theodore Emmerson, along with the sworn testimony of the butler, John Stanton, saying that he witnessed Emmerson ingest the pills on several occasions, as well as the sworn testimony of Peter Manfred, that the suspects interacted with Emmerson, we can easily connect the suspects to Emmerson. And furthermore, the suspects can also be connected as a result of their activities concerning Mrs. Emmerson. That, compiled with the attempted murder of Mariah Emmerson's nephew, and the findings of the subsequent raid on the Church of Blessed Deliverance, the D.A. says that it's a slam dunk, that neither of the suspects will ever see daylight again," explained O'Malley.

"You better take a drink," laughed Phillip. "That was a mouthful."

Sean chuckled and took a long sip of his Green River.

"You know, you could have just said, 'you nailed his ass'," laughed Phillip.

"I haven't said, 'nailed his ass' since I made captain," laughed O'Malley.

Phyllis and Benjamin chuckled as the ate their hotdogs.

Later that day Mariah Emmerson showed up at the Clark offices. Alice brought Mariah into Phillip's office.

"I came in today to thank you and you're fine people for what they've done for me," Mariah told Phillip. "That young man, Duck…well, he might look like a bum, but he is a kind and very considerate young man. His girlfriend, Jackie, is likewise a fine young woman. I can't imagine the strength that it takes to engage a criminal in a gun fight."

"It wasn't her first, though I believe that she never killed anyone before," Phillip returned.

"Nora, Patterson's girlfriend, your secretary, has informed me of the news concerning the prosecution of Corrothers and Gates. I am very pleased," continued Mariah.

"We do what we can," smiled Phillip. "If you don't mind me asking, what about your relationship with your brother's family?"

Mariah face brightened noticeably, "It is as it should be. I was such a fool. I intend to spend so much time with them that they'll be sick of me."

Phillip laughed, "I can't see them ever getting sick of you, Mariah."

Mariah thanked Phillip.

"And now I would like to write you a check for what I owe you," Mariah announced.

"Well, it ain't all that much, I'm afraid," Phillip said. "At best it's only six days work, that is, if I count the days that Duck and Jackie were working on the case before I got involved."

"By all means count them," insisted Mariah.

"I guess that I'll have to refund your nephew's dollar. I can't double bill," Phillip laughed.

Mariah laughed and placed a check on Phillip's desk. Phillip took it in his hands.

"I'm afraid that this is way more than I'm entitled to," Phillip informed.

"Nonsense!" snapped Mariah. "You saved Patterson's life, all my money, and most likely, you saved my own life! Theodore always said that a worker is worthy of his wages. Your people are fine workers, Mr. Clark and they are worthy of every cent, and maybe much more. The amount that is over your customary fee can be given to your employees as a bonus."

"That's very generous, Mrs. Emmerson. I'll do just that," Phillip assured.

"Thank you, Mr. Clark. I wish you and yours well," Mariah offered.

"And the same to you and yours, Mrs. Emmerson," Phillip returned as Mariah turned to leave.

As she walked out of the office, Phillip called after her, "I'm also so very sorry about your husband, Ma'am."

Mariah turned, "So am I, but I don't intend to stop living because of it."

Phillip nodded, "That's the spirit! I did the same thing and never regretted it."